PENGUIN BOOKS

THe TRUTH ABOUT LEO

D__ __d Yelland was born in Yorkshire in 1963. He began
to __ rite poetry as a child but stopped to pursue a dream
of __ eing a journalist. He grew up to edit newspapers in
I__ __don and New York City. This is his first novel.

www.davidyelland.com

THE TRUTH ABOUT LEO

DAVID YELLAND

PENGUIN BOOKS

PENGUIN BOOKS

Published by the Penguin Group
Penguin Books Ltd, 80 Strand, London WC2R ORL, England
Penguin Group (USA) Inc., 375 Hudson Street, New York, New York 10014, USA
Penguin Group (Canada), 90 Eglinton Avenue East, Suite 700, Toronto, Ontario, Canada M4P 2Y3
(a division of Pearson Penguin Canada Inc.)
Penguin Ireland, 25 St Stephen's Green, Dublin 2, Ireland (a division of Penguin Books Ltd)
Penguin Group (Australia), 250 Camberwell Road, Camberwell, Victoria 3124, Australia
(a division of Pearson Australia Group Pty Ltd)
Penguin Books India Pvt Ltd, 11 Community Centre, Panchsheel Park, New Delhi – 110 017, India
Penguin Group (NZ), 67 Apollo Drive, Rosedale, North Shore 0632, New Zealand
(a division of Pearson New Zealand Ltd)
Penguin Books (South Africa) (Pty) Ltd, 24 Sturdee Avenue, Rosebank, Johannesburg 2196, South Africa

Penguin Books Ltd, Registered Offices: 80 Strand, London WC2R ORL, England

www.penguin.com

First published 2010
1

Set in 13/16pt Baskerville by Palimpsest Book Production Limited,
Grangemouth, Stirlingshire
Made and printed in England by Clays Ltd, St Ives plc

British Library Cataloguing in Publication Data
A CIP catalogue record for this book is available from the British Library

ISBN: 978-0-141-33003-7

www.greenpenguin.co.uk

Penguin Books is committed to a sustainable future
for our business, our readers and our planet.
The book in your hands is made from paper
certified by the Forest Stewardship Council.

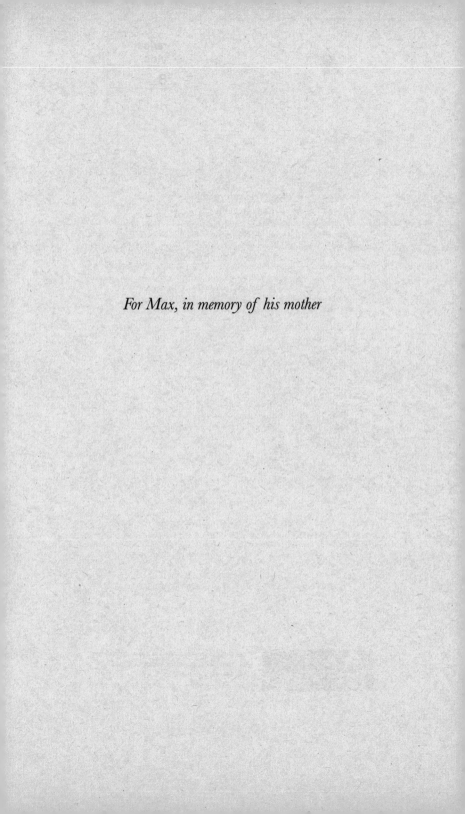

For Max, in memory of his mother

Contents

1. Planet Leo   1

2. The Secret   17

3. A Light Under the Door   32

4. The Hunter in the Night   37

5. On Starfish Nights   44

6. Four Thirty   57

7. Just an Act   65

8. A Sleepless PM   72

9. Disaster!   80

10. Flora's Secret   88

11. Faith Not Sight   97

12. Where Did All the Mums Go?   108

13. Save the Box!   112

14. Lost Property   122

15. The Visitor   133

16. In the Garden   143

17. Lion's Den   163

18. Nan's Story   171

19. Finding Out   185

20. The Counting's Over   195

21. Barnaby's Return   208

22. The Man in the Drive   227

Acknowledgements   239

Author's Note   241

Footfalls echo in the memory
Down the passage which we did not take
Towards the door we never opened
Into the rose-garden.

T. S. Eliot, 'Burnt Norton'

'Better leave the kid alone,' a voice shouted over the noise of the crowd.

Leo felt another hand on his shoulder, looked round and saw a famous smile.

'Thanks, JT,' he whispered, catching a wink from John Terry as they neared the green of the Wembley pitch.

He felt JT's hand on his shoulder again. Firm. Purposeful.

'Do you know why he's getting at you?' the England captain whispered, looking up at the TV cameras in the tunnel, making sure he couldn't be heard. 'Because he knows how good you are.

'Every place you go on that pitch, I'm with you. We're all with you. Understand, son? Don't fear him; don't fear anybody. Out there – we look after each other. OK?'

JT was looking him firm in the eye. He winked again, then turned and walked to his captain's place at the front of the team. By the time the players reached the pitch the noise of the crowd was so loud Leo couldn't think.

In Leo's head, he heard the television commentator. 'And they are singing this young man's name. What a dream this is for the young Leo Rake . . . who today becomes the youngest Englishman to ever play for his country . . . a dream come true for the tragic young man whose mother passed away when he was just eight years old. How proud would she be today, Andy . . .?'

'Well, Steve, I just couldn't find the words for that one, you know. She'd be very proud, I know that much. I know I am. I think the whole country is . . . The whole country will be with this boy today. What was it John Terry called him the other day?'

'JT said he could be the best player the country had ever produced, Andy, a hell of a compliment –'

Somebody *was* pushing his shoulder. But it wasn't JT.

It was Manders.

Leo thought about speaking. But reckoned he could stay in his own world just a few minutes longer.

He looked up at Manders, red rollneck jumper in need of a wash, yellowed teeth and big squashy lips that concertina'd when he talked. And worst of all his black beard streaked with grey, which covered his face, like he had something to hide.

Leo wondered why Manders never cut his beard, or at least trimmed it. It seemed to be allowed to roam free on his face, setting up camp wherever it liked.

He could see the old buffer was jabbering on. Talking rubbish, as usual.

But Leo wasn't listening. Wembley was heating up now. It was time for the national anthems . . . The Germans would be first. He heard the music in his head.

'Duur-dur-dur-duur, dur-dur-dur, duh-*duh* . . .'

Leo tried to hold on to Wembley but the signal was fading. The real world was pulling him back. He was back in the classroom now, with its smells of mouldy trainers and boredom.

He knew they were all laughing at him. Laughing at Manders's skit, which he could tell was all about him. He felt the class's laughter vibrate around him; he knew its rhythm all too well.

Manders towered above him. Once or twice he glanced down at Leo but mostly he was talking to the class, his arms gesticulating wildly.

He was playing to the gallery as usual, enjoying the appreciation of a captive audience. Leo was his straight man, the unwilling other half of a daily double act.

Still Leo didn't listen. He wouldn't. He refused to let them in.

How he hated Manders, he thought, how he hated the lot of them.

He noticed how many whiskers from his rotten beard were stuck on the top of Manders's red scruffy jumper.

As he watched, he saw another detach itself from his beard and cartwheel down his chest before getting caught. He noticed it was black but turned to white at one end, like a badger's.

It was then the sound burst in on him. He couldn't

keep the real world out forever, no matter how hard he tried. Eventually the noise of the world always came rushing in, like when he came up for air in a swimming pool.

'Is there anybody in there?' Manders demanded, pointing at Leo, his head turned away towards his audience.

'Earth to Leo, Earth to Leo: is there anybody there?'

The laughter was stronger now. It had spread, even, to the timid kids, the ones who only laughed when everybody laughed.

Leo tried to let it wash over him, like the breakwaters on Easthampton beach let the waves wash over them.

But Manders's ranting brought him back to reality.

'Is it nice in there?' he was saying, his face pushed close to Leo's. 'Is it nice in there on Planet Leo?'

Leo looked at Manders.

You don't understand me, he thought.

You think you do, but you don't.

Leo felt tired. He always felt tired. If he'd ever woken up brimming with energy, he couldn't remember how it felt.

If only you knew, he thought, looking up at Manders's leering face.

You'd know why I'm late for school, why my homework's never done.

You'd know why I always have the wrong sports kit and why it's never washed.

Then you'd understand, he thought.

Maybe then you'd leave me alone.

But Manders didn't know. Nobody knew. Leo couldn't tell. Not now. Not ever.

Manders wasn't finished.

'Since Mr Rake refuses to speak to us,' he was saying, 'since he prefers to remain on Planet Leo, I guess we will have to think of some special punishment for the inevitable fact that he has obviously left his homework at home again. Until he finds his tongue.'

The laughter was reaching fever pitch.

'You will recall that it was Mr Rake here whose job it was to write up neatly and then post our letter to the Prime Minister. Have you done it, boy?'

Leo muttered his reply, hoping nobody else in class would hear.

'Yes . . . No . . . Sort of, Sir, I . . . er . . .'

But everybody had heard. The class was quiet now, waiting, listening for the next instalment.

'Well, that is a first, even for you, Rake,' Manders boomed. 'The answer to the simple question: "Did you post the letter?" seems to be *yes* and *no*, not to mention *sort of* . . .'

Manders was addressing the class again, warming to his task.

'All you had to do, Rake, was pop it in the post

box. I seem to recall it was a very good letter too.'

A huge hoot of laughter greeted this remark. The back row of the class convulsed. Leo turned to look at them. They were always the ones that laughed the loudest. The trouble-makers. Mary Chesterton and that girl Kerry, who followed her around like a puppy.

Then there was another voice, a kinder voice, cutting through the laughter.

'Why don't you all just shut up!' the voice was saying. 'It's not as if any of you ever have an idea as good as Leo's.'

It was Flora, sat at the next desk.

When she spoke, the class hushed for a fraction of time, but Leo knew the way it worked.

'Oo – er. It's the weirdo's little girlfriend!'

How he hated Mary Chesterton. Then she and the Kerry girl began to chant.

'Now–we–know–your–*boy*–friend!'

Leo stole a glance at Flora. She was smiling at him. That was why he liked her. She could always cheer him up. She seemed to understand.

So what if she was a girl. He didn't care.

He could tell her anything. Well, not quite anything. Not yet. And, anyway, she'd only been at Pier Road a term.

Leo liked the way her hair was always spiked up, even though she didn't seem to ever comb it. It was cut short and blonde.

She was looking up at Manders, no longer smiling: her pale blue eyes were stern. She was trying to make a point.

Manders positioned himself between their two desks.

He was trying to be serious, trying to calm the disorder he had caused himself.

His arms were folded. His lips were pursed.

He's thinking of what to say next, Leo thought. He's trying to work out how to shut the class up.

Leo watched Manders stretch his body up, arching his back, trying to be as tall as he could. Pulling rank on a bunch of kids.

'Thank you, Flora Long, for your contribution to the proceedings,' Manders mocked, leaning down towards her.

'It was all Leo's idea, Sir. That's all I'm saying. I mean it was his idea to write to the Prime Minister in the first place. To ask him to open the school library, Sir. Because you used to teach him here, Sir. Like you said. In this very class.'

Leo watched Flora. Saw how she was winding Manders round her little finger. Praising him. Flattering him. Making him feel important.

He was stuffed up even more now, like a robin on a Boxing Day bird-table, packed with pickings.

'Well, I did use to teach Mr Green. Yes, he was a pupil of mine . . .' Manders said, for some reason speaking all posh and high and mighty. 'Or Barnaby, as of course I knew him way before he became Prime Minister . . .'

Manders was laughing to himself as if he'd told the funniest joke in the world, his shoulders moving up and down.

'I mean, Sir, it's supposed to be a joint letter, isn't it?' Flora carried on, Manders putty in her hands. 'From us all to him. It's a joint letter from our class to him . . . so we can just write it again, can't we?'

Flora's hands were inside her school bag, searching for something.

'I've got the beginnings of it here. I wrote a lot of it down,' she went on, finding a notebook and fishing it out.

Manders stood bemused, seemingly unable to stop her.

Quickly she opened the book up and began reading.

'Dear Prime Minister. We are pupils in Class 5M at Pier Road Primary School and our teacher, Mr Manders, has told us that you used to be a pupil at our school . . .'

Manders had begun to calm down and, at the mention of his name, calmed further, mollified.

'Carry on,' he said matter-of-factly, turning to walk back towards the board.

Flora grinned at Leo, triumphant.

'We know that Mr Manders was your favourite teacher when you were here –'

Manders was wagging his finger. 'Oh, I don't think we need to put that . . .'

He paused.

'Always be modest, children. Remember that.'

When he turned back to the board Leo and Flora exchanged glances, their eyebrows raised.

'Modest. *Manders!*' Flora mouthed, her hands held up beside her head, pretending it was giant-sized.

'Carry on, Miss Long,' the teacher growled, his back still turned.

'. . . and that the school didn't have a proper library, just the bookshelves in the corridor. You will be pleased to know we are about to open a brand-new library and we are all very excited –'

Manders had turned and was interrupting.

'*Pleased*, Miss Long, I think we say *pleased*, not "excited". Don't you? This is a library, not a pop concert.'

'– pleased,' Flora continued, ignoring a fresh ripple of laughter from the class. 'We know that as Prime Minister you are very busy but we were wondering if you would like to come back to your old school to open the library officially . . .'

Flora folded up her letter, winking at Leo, laughter bubbling up inside her.

'That's as far as I got, Sir,' she smiled.

Manders ignored her and instead surveyed the class, his piggy little eyes finally resting on Leo once again.

'Right,' he barked, 'that's not a bad start. But we still have to deal with the letter-loser, don't we . . . Have you got anything to say for yourself, Rake?'

'Yes,' Leo whispered, looking up, knowing that this time he had to tell the truth.

After all, they might find out. If his stupid plan worked.

'I've kind of . . . I mean I've already sort of sent the letter, I mean I think I have . . .'

The laughter in the class stopped, suddenly. They wanted to hear this for themselves. This was too good to miss.

Even Flora was looking at Leo oddly. She didn't know the trick he'd tried.

'Let's get this straight, shall we, Rake? You *think* you've "kind of" sent the letter, but you're not sure . . .' Manders said, pronouncing his words slowly for maximum effect. 'Even by your pathetic standards that's one for the record books. It really is.'

Manders arrived back in front of Leo's desk, leering at him, his tongue stuck out to the side, a snapshot of a stupid person's studied concentration.

Leo realized something then. He realized that this was what Manders enjoyed best, humiliating him.

Worse still – this was probably what he *did* best. It was Manders that was pathetic, not him.

But knowing all that wasn't going to help him, because Manders was the teacher and he was the kid. He was just going to have to put up with it.

Manders rounded on him again.

'Would you care to clarify, Rake? In words of one syllable. Have you sent this letter or not? I think we're all a tad confused.'

Flora was looking at him as confused as the rest of them and he knew why. She'd tried to save him and then he'd messed things up. He had to explain.

When Leo spoke, it was in a whisper.

'I did send it, Sir. I emailed it. Last night.'

The class began to laugh again, but Manders silenced them with a wave of his arm.

'You *emailed* the Prime Minister, did you, Rake?' he said, incredulous. 'What address did you send it to, boy wonder – pm@planetleo.com?'

Leo opened his mouth to reply but decided there was no point. He *had* emailed it. That was true. He'd done it from his own email address too. The one Dad had let him set up on the surgery computer.

But he'd guessed the Prime Minister's email address from the official website. It was just a stab in the dark, really. He knew it wouldn't get through.

So Manders was right. He was an idiot. He was a total failure. Maybe they were *all* right.

Manders had turned to address the class again.

'OK, all of you. We will ignore this boy and carry on as follows. You all heard Flora Long. I'm sure you took notes. By tomorrow I want you all to have your versions of the letter to the Prime Minister and tomorrow we will pick the best one.'

He paused, eyeing Flora.

'We will *post* that one to 10 Downing Street, which – as the brighter sparks among you may know – is the official residence of Mr Barnaby Green, who now runs the country and used to – heaven help him – sit in one of these very seats in this very classroom.'

When Manders paused for a second time, Leo knew he was thinking of a way to have another go at him. Leo could tell. It was the way the teacher's gaze had gone from Leo to Flora and back again; it was like there was unfinished business.

'Although, looking at *some* people in this class, I doubt history is going to repeat itself any time soon.'

Manders now stood in front of the two of them.

'What do you think, Rake? Do you think you stand much chance of making anything of your life at the rate you're going? Maybe you'll even get to school on time tomorrow. Maybe a miracle will befall us. Why *are* you late for school every day, Rake? Maybe I should have a word with your mum . . .'

Now Leo was angry. Really angry. The kind of anger that feels like something molten inside you, the kind that needs letting out. But he didn't let it out. Instead he sat paralysed, his heart beating harder and harder.

Then he heard Flora.

She spoke quietly, her pale cheeks suddenly a rosy pink.

'Don't you know, Mr Manders? Leo hasn't got a mum. She died two years ago. It was before I was here, Sir, but surely *you* remember it?'

Manders froze, his sneer contorted, his eyes suddenly panicky.

In an instant, though, he seemed to regain his composure.

The class was still and silent, as if under a spell. Leo could see they were all as appalled by Manders as he was – but they were fascinated too. They wanted to see how far he would go. For a moment Leo thought the silence would never end.

'I think we had better separate you two,' Manders said in a calm voice, trying to pretend nothing had happened. 'Flora will sit at the front of class. Change over to the desk next to Richards. *Now!*'

Flora didn't protest.

She slid her chair back, its scraping the only sound in class. Slowly she walked to the front, her shoes clip-clipping, then the scraping of the chair.

The bell rang and suddenly the spell was broken.

The crescendo of chairs being pushed back and the eruption of chattering signalling the end of a day.

It was home time.

But Leo never really wanted to go home. Not that anybody knew. He'd kept that secret well. The biggest secret of all.

Instead Leo was back in Leo's World. It was the second half of the Germany game.

'We're into the last ten minutes here at Wembley in the vital World Cup qualifier,' the commentator gushed. 'And England are on the attack. Rooney with a fabulous ball to Joe Cole and now – oh, and here comes the schoolboy, Rake . . . he's broken through the Germans' defence, he takes one touch, two touches . . . three touches, he shoots . . . **G-O-A-L!** RAKE SCORES FOR ENGLAND!'

2
The Secret

Leo pushed open the low white gate with the sign on it marked 'Surgery' and walked up the path to his front door.

Dad's surgery hours would be over already. They seemed to get shorter and shorter with every year since Mum died.

Leo paused in front of the door, wondering if Dad was home. The house was silent, its windows showing no signs of life at all.

Headlights from a passing car lit up the darkened house, catching a small brass plaque fixed on the wall next to Leo's front door:

Dr Tom Rake MB Ch.B. (London)

Leo shrugged. *Dr Tom Rake.* If only all of Easthampton saw what he saw, knew what he knew.

It was like there were two dads. The dad everybody in Easthampton thought they knew – and then the real dad. The one only he and Mum knew.

Only there was no Mum now. Only him.

Leo rang the bell.

He never knew which dad he'd see. Or even if there'd be a dad at all.

He rang the bell a second time.

Was Dad home? He might be. He could be. Leo just knew one thing for sure: everything was always uncertain. He never quite knew what he was going to find.

True, all the lights were out. But sometimes when the lights were out he'd still be home. Like he was hiding.

Why didn't Dad just give him his own key? After all, he knew where it was hidden anyway. It was because Dad wanted to pretend. Pretend he was always home and always let Leo in. Just like he pretended about everything.

Leo listened for the shuffling of feet inside, but none came.

He bent down, took the key from its hiding-place under the raggedy doormat and unlocked the door.

Once inside, Leo took off his coat and hung it on one of the pegs in the hall.

He didn't know why he was bothering being so tidy. Dad's jacket was a roughly crumpled heap on the floor, with all his other coats and scarves. It was a mess. Everything was such a mess.

He cupped his hands. 'H-e-l-l-o-o,' he shouted, moving swiftly through the empty sitting-room into the kitchen.

But inside was only silence.

Sometimes he'd find Dad asleep on the sofa in the sitting-room. But he wasn't there today.

Other times he'd be asleep on his bed, even in the afternoon. Dad did all kinds of things at odd times. He didn't live like normal people.

Leo ran up the stairs to check. Dad's bedroom door was open slightly. But there was no Dad. There was nothing but an unmade bed and the ever-present stink of cigarettes.

How could a doctor smoke cigarettes? Leo had long since stopped trying to work that one out. He knew that Dad knew they were bad for him. He knew they would kill him. Yet still he smoked.

But that wasn't the worst thing. It wasn't the thing that worried Leo most.

It was what Dad drank.

He'd been at it again too. Leo could smell it.

As he padded down the stairs, he saw the signs. They were all there. All on show in the sitting-room as it came into full view, step by step.

Today there were two bottles.

They were on the low table in the middle of the room. One was empty, the other had a bit left in it.

Leo registered the make of the booze at a glance. He knew all the makes. He knew the vodkas and the gins, the whiskies, the whole shooting match of hooch. Each spelled a slight variation on chaos for him, a gradient of hell.

Some were stronger than the others. He could tell from the numbers on the side.

But they all meant the same thing to Leo. They meant a dadless dad.

They meant him having to cope on his own. They meant covering up.

They meant lies on top of lies.

Leo picked the two bottles up and made for the kitchen. He examined their labels. *Vodka.*

The brand was called *VLADIVOSTI!*. The letters were set out as if they were Russian, with the D in the 'VLAD' a jaunty wrong way round.

Once he'd seen an advert in a magazine for Vladivosti – full of happy people, all smiling and having a good time.

It wasn't like that when Dad drank the stuff. When he drank Vladivosti, he was on his own, hidden behind curtains. In Leo's house the curtains were almost always closed, no matter what the time of day.

Leo threw the empty bottle into the bin in the corner. Then he picked the second one up and swished the remains down the kitchen sink, holding his nose as he did so, zapping it down the plughole with spurts of water.

Then he thought about the others.

The other bottles.

The hidden ones.

The bottles Dad smuggled away in the house for later on when he came home.

Leo set about finding them. He knew all the usual hiding-places by heart. He had them all mapped out in his head, room by room, cupboard by cupboard, secret hiding-place by secret hiding-place.

Like a detective searching a crime scene, he checked the kitchen cupboards one by one. Dad could be crafty. Once he'd found a bottle wrapped in a tea-towel at the back of the sink.

But there was nothing there today.

He tried the downstairs loo. Gingerly he lifted up the cistern top and peered inside. Empty. But this too had been a watery hiding-place.

It was only then, as he was about to leave the loo, that he noticed the boiler's white metal door was unlocked.

He was sure it was usually closed on some kind of catch.

Though metal, the door was light and easy to open.

And there they were!

The night's haul.

There were two of them tonight. He could see their outline in the plastic supermarket bag stuffed between the boiler's copper pipes.

It wasn't difficult to get at the bag, which was tied up at the top in an untidy bow.

Inside were two vodka bottles – each with a red screw-top still undisturbed.

He examined them, turning the bottles and reading the labels. He knew that vodka didn't really come from Russia anyway. That it was all fibs. Sure enough, when he rotated the bottle again, he saw the give-away words.

Distilled in UK.

Russian! As if! And anyway he'd heard on the radio once that some Russians drank so much of the stuff they died in the winter streets. They got so drunk they fell asleep and never woke up. Some advert! Leo thought. But then the grown-up world seemed, to him, to be full of fibs and craziness. Things everybody knew but nobody said. Like there was some big agreement they'd all signed up to. Maybe there was! Maybe that was what they meant by 'growing up'.

He looked again at the bottle, at the small writing down the label's side. It gave the strength of the booze. He'd always done this, from being really young. He'd learned something else too. The stronger the percentage of alcohol, the worse Dad would be when he got home.

ABV 43 per cent.

Leo's pulse raced. He didn't know what the letters meant exactly, but he knew that the higher the number was, the worse things got. Most of Dad's booze was forty not forty-three, so this stuff was three per cent stronger than normal. That was super-strength.

He had to hide them.

He had to try to keep them from his dad.

The way Leo figured it, if Dad couldn't find the bottles maybe he'd give up and go to bed. He had to give it a go.

He remembered when it used to work. Dad would come home and think he'd misplaced them. He'd crash around and finally fall asleep.

Only Dad had got more determined recently. He didn't give up so easily.

Leo tried to focus. He would hide these somewhere Dad would never look. He would hide them in his room, in his own clothes cupboard.

Leo was just climbing the stairs when the phone rang.

The ringing filled the empty house and somehow made its emptiness more marked and scary.

He stopped as still as a mouse, holding the bottles nestled in his arms, making sure they didn't drop and crash to the floor.

The answerphone kicked in.

'You have reached the home of Dr Tom Rake,'

his dad's voice said, all doctor-like. This was Dad's official voice, his voice for the outside world, one that didn't slur and seem all slowed-up, one that made sense.

'If you wish to call the surgery, please call Easthampton 541907. If it is an emergency, either call 999 or the hospital on 555444. Otherwise please leave a message after the tone.'

Leo stood, staring at the machine on the hall table, waiting.

'Tommy . . .' said the voice at the other end of the line. 'Are you there, Tommy?'

It was Nan. For a second Leo thought of grabbing the phone. Maybe today was the day he would tell her what was going on. That Dad wasn't there. That he was never there. That he was always drunk. That Leo had just found the bottles hidden in the boiler in the downstairs loo and that things like this happened every day.

But he knew that would be no use. Once he had tried to tell her. But she'd brushed him off. He remembered the way Nan had looked at him that day. Like it was all his fault. Like telling the truth was the one thing you weren't supposed to do.

He'd learned a few things from that. He'd learned grown-ups sometimes prefer big fat lies. That they sometimes just pretend things are all right even when they're not.

Nan was still speaking.

'Hello, Tommy. I was just wondering how you were, love. I haven't heard from you for a bit . . . Everything all right, son? I know what it's like, what with the surgery and everything, but give us a bell, won't you? Maybe at the weekend? I heard you had to close up a few days last week cos you were ill.

'How's that boy of yours? I don't know what we're going to do with him, Tommy. He's just like his mum, he is, lives in his own little world. He takes after her, mark my words. He'll be trouble when he's older . . . Anyway, Tommy, got to go now. Give me a ring, like I say, when you can . . .'

There was the sound of clicking and confusion as Nan worked out how to put down her own phone. Then she was gone.

Well, there it was, thought Leo, official! Now he knew what he'd long suspected. Nan had never liked Mum. Not really. And it sounded like she had it in for *him* too.

Nan wouldn't have a bad word said about Dad. Not him! Not the doctor. But she always seemed to think the worst of Leo. Just like she had of Mum.

Was she just stupid? Or was she blind? Leo didn't know. He couldn't work it out. All he did know was that he wasn't getting any help from her. That was for sure.

Leo carried on up the stairs, making for his bedroom.

Maybe it was better that no one did know. He'd seen what happened to kids like him on the telly. Seen what they did with families with dads like his, dads who were always drunk.

Social services would come. They'd come to the house if they knew. They'd work things out all right. It wouldn't take them long. They'd see the bottles. The smell, the stink. Then where would he be?

In a children's home, that's where. Or fostered off with people he didn't know.

That was the one thing he had to avoid. He was certain about that, because if that happened that would mean the worst thing of all. He'd have no dad either then. No hope. He'd be on his own. But if no one knew there was always at least a chance that things would get better.

He could still see the old dad sometimes. The dad he loved. It was like he was hiding deep inside but couldn't get out.

Then there was the other reason he had to stay in the house. Mum's room. If he was taken away, he'd never get to see inside Mum's room ever again. And there was no way he was going to let that happen.

Not that he'd been in Mum's room any time recently. Truth be known, he hadn't been in since Mum had died, worse luck.

Dad wouldn't allow him. It was out of bounds. Whenever he went up to the top floor of the house and tried the door – which he did almost every day – it was always locked.

But somehow Leo never gave up. He knew one day it would be open. One day he would get back inside.

Just like he knew he would go and check again now. When he'd hidden the bottles, he would mount the stairs to the top floor and try the lock.

Just in case.

Leo liked his own room. He liked its smallness. The way he could lie on his bed and see every part of it and know he was safe.

He liked the posters on his walls. Especially the one with the flowers Mum had put up for him. He liked the painters Mum said had come from France; he liked their pictures of the flowers in the fields.

Mum had painted flowers too. But her paintings were all upstairs and hidden. So he had to imagine them, magic them up in Leo's World.

There were footie posters too. One of the England squad, another of Shaun Wright-Phillips. He was small like Leo but he always came out on top. Leo thought he was cool.

He felt safe in his room. There was a word he'd learned that explained the way he thought of it.

Sanctuary! That's what this place was, his very own sanctuary. It was his hideaway. Where he kept his things.

The bedroom's small sash window was open to the early evening. Leo went over and looked out. The trees were leafier now, suddenly plump, silhouettes of spring against the sea.

He could hear the sea smashing into Easthampton's pebbly beach. It was like a friendly giant taking spaced-out breaths, powerful but calm as well. Comfy like a friend.

But the garden still made him sad. Since Mum had died there'd been nobody to look after it. Once the garden had been full of colour, full of life. But no longer.

These days everyday things made him sad. Like empty houses and empty bottles. Like memories of other times.

Leo picked up a photograph in a cut-glass frame. It was his favourite because it had been Mum's favourite too. Even though *he* was in it: Dad. But it wasn't the dad he knew now in the photo; it was the old dad. The dad he loved. He had his arms around Mum. And there in the middle was Leo. A happy boy with happy parents. The normal boy he longed to be.

Mum had loved the picture. For years it had hung on a hook in the hall, the first thing you saw when you came into the house. But the hook had been bare and empty for as long as he could remember now. The picture had been in *his* room, instead, leaning next to the lamp on his bedside table. A precious refugee from happier times.

It hadn't always been like this.

Leo could still remember better times. If he tried really hard, he could remember a more normal dad.

Like when they used to play football in the garden.

He remembered the bald patches on the lawn where the goals had been!

Best of all he remembered their special game, the one they'd invented, the one they'd played even in the dark with the garden floodlit by the outside lights.

'Pyjama football', Dad had called it. Leo remembered him coming down the stairs. It must have been early in the morning in winter time.

'Stick your boots on, Lion – prepare for defeat!' Dad would yell.

They'd play in the mornings back then. And after dark as well.

But that was another life, another Dad. Another boy, not him.

There were no bald patches now because there was no football. The grass left rampant.

Night was approaching. He felt hungry. Soon he

would have to go downstairs and find some food.
Maybe there was still a pizza in the freezer.

But first: hide the bottles. He'd tried everywhere
in the past. But lately Dad kept finding them.

He wondered why he bothered. Why not just leave
them where Dad did? Leave him to it . . .

Leo pulled open the big doors of his cupboard.
Everything was in there. A discarded pile of
unwashed clothes. His spare school clothes and his
normal clothes, all mixed up. He picked up one of
his shirts, noticing he'd outgrown it. He'd outgrown
most things in the cupboard.

Mum had always bought his clothes and Dad
never bothered. It was as if his whole life had gone
on hold the moment Mum had died.

Leo sometimes felt he was in a time machine which
had stuck at the precise moment Mum had died.
These days he had to rely on Mrs York to wash his
things and put them away. And some weeks she
hardly seemed to bother.

He tried to shake the thoughts away. There were
things that needed to be done. He had to concentrate.
He tried his best, screwing up his face and looking
at the pile of unwashed shirts and socks and pants.

Wasn't it obvious? The big ugly pile was to his
advantage. Quickly he took the bottles and pushed
them into the pile, hiding them deep in its smelly
middle.

Leo closed the cupboard. That would have to do for now.

Now to test the lock. Now to see if Mum's room was open.

3

A Light Under the Door

Even before he mounted the stairs Leo knew it was hopeless. Mum's room was bound to be locked.

But he'd try it. Just in case.

When he got to the door, he gripped the door handle and made a silent wish: *Let it be open this time, so I can see inside.*

He could picture it in his mind's eye, see every detail.

He could see the French windows at the far end, open to Mum's small balcony that overlooked the town. He remembered how the sea breeze billowed the see-through curtains.

He saw Mum's paintings framed on the walls. Paintings of the sea and paintings of flowers; pictures etched on to his memory of long-gone summer days when everything had seemed all right. Days with Mum he'd hoped would last forever.

He saw too the real flowers. Mum's chamomile flowers. The ones she grew on the side, on what she always called her 'chamomile sideboard'. How it groaned with the weight of the yellow and white flowers, all lined up in oblong trays.

Then there were Mum's books. Hundreds of books. There were so many of them that the shelves were overflowing and they were stacked on the floor and near the windows. Books on travelling and gardening. Cookery books. Novels. Her poetry books. Books she'd bought for Leo.

Then he pictured the very best thing of all. The Memory Box. The box Mum had made especially for him. The box that Dad had never let him have.

Dad never talked about the Memory Box. Except once. One night when he was drunk.

Dad had said it would be too upsetting for Leo to see the box; that the room was just full of things that would bring back sad memories.

Didn't Dad understand that the memories were there anyway? And that some of them weren't sad at all? But they were his memories and everything in the room was a part of that. He had a *right* to go in there.

He knew exactly where the Memory Box was: in the bottom drawer of the chamomile sideboard.

He could almost feel it, big and heavy, so wide he always had to stretch his arms to carry it. It was covered in shiny stones they'd bought together in the craft shop in the town.

He remembered making it with Mum, remembered how they'd painted it in reds and yellows, greens and blues. Great sweeps of colour. He pictured the photo of him and Mum they had glued on the top. He remembered how they had stuck it next to the words they'd painted on the top – words in big red letters in Mum's writing – *LEO'S MEMORY BOX*.

Leo could almost reach out and touch it. He could feel the brightly coloured stones – what he and Mum had jokingly called their 'jewels'.

They weren't really jewels. Not real, expensive ones. But, to him and Mum, they were the most valuable jewels in the world and they had stuck them on the sides with superglue. He remembered how they'd glinted in the sunlight.

He tried to remember all the things inside. There were the pictures of Mum and him, even ones of all three of them like the picture in his room. Photos from when Dad was Dad. Ones when Dad's face was normal and not all fat and red. Ones when there was white in Dad's eyes, not bloodshot red. Ones from a time so long ago Leo sometimes thought he'd dreamed it up.

There were other things too. Mum's precious diaries. Her favourite books. Black notebooks with leather covers and shoe-lace bookmarks. Her paintings, all rolled up.

Then there were the birthday cards. He knew they

existed. He knew they were in the box. Mum had left him a birthday card, or even a letter, for each birthday up until he was eighteen. He knew that because she'd told him.

But he was ten now. He'd had two birthdays since she'd died.

And no card from Mum.

That was what made it even worse. Mum had meant him to have those cards. And they were so close, just the other side of the door.

It was time to test the lock!

Leo turned the doorknob and pushed.

The door was locked.

Just like it was always locked.

Leo's gaze dropped to the foot of the door where all the marks were. The ones he'd rather forget. All the marks he'd left kicking the door in frustration. Some had taken away the paint. Others were mere scuff marks where he'd kicked out a dirty shoe in frustration.

But this time he didn't kick the door. He knew it was useless.

Leo was just about to turn around and walk down the stairs when something caught his eye. Or at least he thought it did.

It was coming from under the door. Something odd. Something that just couldn't be. . . Was he *seeing* things?

No. He was sure he had seen it. He bent down and looked at the bottom of Mum's door.

There was some kind of light. A glowing kind of light. And it was coming from inside the room.

Then it was gone in a flash. Gone as quickly as it had come.

4

The Hunter in the Night

It was the middle of the night when the sound of crashing on the stairs woke Leo.

He lay still, curled up, his eyes fixed on the back of the bedroom door.

Breathless, he waited. He waited and he listened.

Dad was charging up the stairs. He was shouting at the top of his voice but Leo couldn't make out what he was saying.

All he knew was that the whole house seemed to be shaking; as if a giant's boots were hitting each stair.

And he knew what he wanted too. The bottles. He would be hunting for the bottles.

Then Dad's wild silhouette burst through his door, throwing it open, smashing it with a loud crack against the bottom of his bed.

Dad's hands fumbled for the light-switch, clawing at the wall. Leo just had time to shield his face before blinding light flooded the room – and then, through his fingers, he could see his father.

There was a redness all about him: his face crimson, his eyes bloodshot and wild. The redness was beneath the sweat that formed on his forehead and in the dimple below his bottom lip. His white shirt, worn for the day's surgery, was open to his midriff, its tails hanging out; his braces swung at his knees.

And he was still shouting.

'We both know,' he sneered, and spat his words, 'what you've got hidden. Do you hear me?'

Dad bent down over the bed, his unshaven face butted close. Leo could smell the stink of drink and cigarettes.

This time he's worse, Leo thought. This time he's really lost it.

This was different. It was like it wasn't Dad at all. It was somebody else, somebody scarier.

Leo realized he had no idea what would happen next. Even worse, he knew Dad didn't either. It was as if Dad wasn't in his own body, like something else had grabbed the controls.

It was his eyes that really scared Leo. There was a blankness there like they weren't plugged in.

Suddenly Dad was grabbing him by the shoulders, hauling him up and out of bed.

Then he was shaking him, shaking him hard, his hands gripping Leo's arms and pinning them against his body.

'You're hurting me!' Leo tried to scream, but somehow only a whisper came out. He tried again.

'Please stop! DAD!'

Leo felt his head snap back and then forward like a child's doll. Fear really gripped him now. Dad had never hurt him before. Was he so angry now he wouldn't know how to stop?

Dad was shouting so loud Leo couldn't think. The noise stung his ears and tears stung his eyes.

'Where have you put them?' Dad snarled. 'I can't find them anywhere. You know what I mean . . . You know why I'm here . . .'

Then suddenly Leo was falling. Dad had let him go.

The back of his head hit a bedpost – *thwack!* – a sickening smack. The pain spread out like spilled milk.

He cried out but his cry was a whisper once again, lost amid Dad's screams.

'COME ON! Give them to me . . . COME ON!'

Leo's hand went to his head and he saw there was blood.

He glanced again at Dad, who stood above him like a giant now. He had raised his clenched hand; an insanity in his eyes.

He's going to hit me, Leo thought.

But when the fist came down it struck his bookshelves instead.

It sent his favourite football books and his CDs flying into the air.

Then Dad's fist was raised again, his eyes still blazing.

Suddenly Leo started fighting back. He had no choice. He stood up on the bed and was attacking, pummelling his fists on Dad like a bad fighter in the playground.

He was desperate; he didn't care.

And now it was him that was screaming.

'I won't tell you! I won't because I don't want you to find them! I don't want you to drink them!' he yelled.

Uncertainty hung in the room. Dad was shaking now and his face, when it turned to Leo, was a hunter's face, without feelings, hard and terrifying.

'You need to tell me and you need to tell me now . . .' he began. There was a fury in Dad's voice, an unappealing childish whining. But there was violence in it too. Leo played his last card.

'Please, Dad . . .' Leo said, his voice low now, almost a whisper. 'Please don't drink any more tonight . . . Please . . .'

Suddenly Dad's voice softened. 'Just tell me where they are and I'll be gone.'

Leo was silent. He had no more cards to play.

'I'm going to speak slowly so you understand.' Dad was talking now, not shouting, but there was cold anger in his voice. 'You have hidden something that is mine. I know you hide them. I know you play games. I know what you do and I want it to end now! Do you understand?'

Dad gripped his arms and shook him. 'What the hell's the matter with you, Leo? Why do you have to cause all these problems? It's the middle of the night . . .'

Leo saw desperation flare in his father's eyes. Worse still, he knew why. All Dad wanted was one more drink. He loved the drink more than anything. He loved the drink more than him.

Dad was shouting louder now.

'Why do you do this, Leo?' he yelled. 'Why do we have to play this game?'

Leo searched Dad's face for the father he loved, but he could not see him; he was not there.

Leo had no fight left in him. 'Because I don't want you to have another drink, Dad,' he whispered, 'I just want . . . I just want you to go to bed.'

Instantly, Leo sensed he had crossed a line. He watched his dad's eyes roam the room, searching for ways to hurt him.

Dad's gaze settled on Leo's prized possession, the cut-glass framed picture of the two of them with Mum.

Dad seized it, holding it high in triumph.

'NO! DAD! NO! PLEASE DON'T!' Leo leaped

to stop him but Dad was too quick. He hurled the picture against the wall. Its finely etched border exploded and shards of glass rained around the room.

The photo, released from its frame, wafted gently to land face-down on the floor. Leo made to grab it but his father's bulk pushed him back on to his bed.

'You can forget about HER!' Dad shouted, his voice anguished and hysterical. 'She's dead, don't you understand? She can't help you and she can't help me . . .'

Dad began to cry, his anger turning to self-pity. His body heaved, his breathing jagged and loud. He whispered, sobbing:

'Nobody cares about me . . .'

He collapsed on to the bed, his head in his hands.

This was what always happened. Dad always cried and Leo always had to comfort him, like he was the dad and his father was the child.

Leo put his arms around him as best he could. But he felt clumsy and uncomfortable. He stroked Dad's back, watching how his body heaved up and down.

'I care, Dad, I care . . . and that's why –' He glanced at his cupboard in the corner. The door had opened in the mêlée. 'I don't want you to . . . to –'

Leo realized his mistake as soon as he had made it. Dad had followed his line of sight and was off the bed in an instant, burrowing inside the cupboard like a fox down a hole, flinging great piles of clothes out over his shoulder.

Leo heard the clink of glass and when Dad turned round he was jubilant, wild-eyed like an animal that has found its kill. He stood up clutching the bottles and stepped away from the cupboard, swaying, as though he had lost his footing. Leo saw that he gripped the bottles closer to him, as if they would help him balance. He staggered towards Leo, crowding him, his foul-breath stink in Leo's face again.

'What do you want from me?' he growled.

Leo sat hunched on his bed and wrapped his arms around his knees. He tucked his head down and began to rock, ever so gently, back and forth. For a second Leo's mind was blank. He had nothing to say.

When he did speak, his voice was muffled, his chin on his chest as he rocked.

'I just want my dad back,' he whispered.

'I just want a normal dad.'

Chapter 5
On Starfish Nights

For a time Leo lay still, fearing Dad might come back.

One, two, three . . . He began to count.

Soon he reached 100. He didn't stop . . .

Slowly Leo felt his body become less tense and begin to relax; the throbbing in his head subsided.

An eerie silence hung over the house, an uncertain peace, the kind of peace that might not last for long.

It was always like this. Sometimes he thought the noisy nights were better than the quiet ones. At least he knew what was happening. He could see the danger.

Leo tried to snuggle up. But he knew he wouldn't sleep just yet. So instead he did what he always did: he checked out Leo's World – the world inside his head.

He tried to think of Mum.

It wasn't that he thought he could wish her back

to life. He knew that would never happen. But he could escape into his mind and picture her, just one more time.

Mum is in her room upstairs. She's near the end, in the time beyond pretending, when she had talked to him about all the big things.

He can see her now.

She's in her favourite rocking-chair, her tartan rug tucked around her, her eyes a tawny brown just like his own.

He sees her skin. It seems greyer now, pinched and drawn.

They sit together on the tiny balcony overlooking the higgledy slopes of Easthampton roofs, red and huddled and cosy by the sea.

Above the roofs are black-smudged yellow chimney-pots with seagull sentries standing guard.

They can see the sea from here. A band of pale blue beyond it all. Easthampton's pier sticks into the blue like a lollipop; and then, nearer, the breakwaters box up the sea into side-by-side squares.

The sea frowns, furrowed into worry-lines.

In the middle of the town stands the lighthouse, as if stuck down randomly between the houses.

Even now, in the heat of a summer's day, its red light beats like a tiny heart, always there, never resting, preparing for the night.

It comforts Leo, like it comforts the fishermen at

sea. It makes him feel safe like them, which he knows is never really safe at all.

Below the balcony at the far end of the garden are Mum's roses. Her rose garden. He sees a medley of bright colours, crowding around the fine-cut grass.

Beyond the rose garden is the hedge and then rolling common land. South Green. All lush grass and criss-crossed paths down to the sea.

And before the sea are the beach huts. A row of colours in the hazy distance.

He hears the sounds of Easthampton's summer. The cries of laughing children hang in the air.

For them this is a normal day.

Leo looks at Mum as she rocks steadily in her rocking-chair, her face turned to the sea.

He notices another change. Her face has grown a silvery down which shimmers in the sun.

It seems to Leo that Mum is like a Russian doll, each day a new mum emerging from the old. Only each mum is smaller, more fragile than the last.

And although he prays she'll stay, although he prays she'll linger on, he knows she has few Russian dolls left now to shed.

Next to Mum is a metal pole with blinking lights and switches halfway up. It has been left by the doctor and has to be with her night and day. Two tubes go from the pole to the back of Mum's hand and more taped-up tubes.

'Lion, be a darling and get the Memory Box for me, will you?' Mum asks, the breeze blowing her hair across her face.

Far below, a child shrieks, his kite lost to the mercy of the sea.

'Do I have to get it now?' he says.

Mum just nods.

'You know where it is,' she says, 'under the chamomile sideboard.'

Mum's room is full of her precious things. Her pictures hang on the walls, paintings of flowers everywhere.

Then there are the real flowers. They're everywhere too, cluttering the room. Flowers in pots on the floor, on tables and on the sides. Ones she's starting off as seedlings and others ready for the garden.

Mum's 'chamomile sideboard' is a white-topped chest of drawers, creaking with the distinctive yellow and white flowers.

Underneath, in the bottom drawer of the hefty sideboard, is where the Memory Box is kept.

For as long as Leo can remember, he has known about the box. He can never remember a time when Mum wasn't ill, when adults didn't check he'd gone before they spoke about her health.

But Leo had heard everything. He knew the truth.

Mum would die and then he'd be alone and that was that. He'd always known.

Leo bends down, pulls opens the drawer and wraps his arms around the precious box. His Memory Box. It is heavy and the weight shifts within it as things move, making it difficult to carry.

With some effort Leo carries it through the French windows and is back on the balcony. The coloured stones stuck on the side dig into him, but he doesn't mind.

'Put it down – here – on the side table,' Mum says.

As he sits down, Mum turns her face to his.

'Is there anything you want to ask me, Lion?' she asks.

'You mean about the box?'

'About anything. Remember how we used to talk about anything and everything. You know . . . on starfish nights . . .'

Leo misses starfish nights. Nights when he'd creep into Mum's bed only to stick his arms and legs out like a starfish in his sleep – so wide, in fact, that Mum would wake him saying she couldn't sleep.

But now the stick with the wires follows her like a bad ghost. Its wires get in the way and there are no more starfish nights.

Leo has taken the lid off the box and is looking inside.

Inside there are framed pictures in bubblewrap. But he recognizes the images through the bubbles.

There are Mum's diaries in plastic see-through

bags and her paintings rolled up and tied. There are her favourite books, her poetry. Things for when he's older.

Then he sees his birthday envelopes addressed to him, each with a number in the top right corner.

Mum had shown them to him before.

Leo knew what the numbers signified. They were his birthdays. Each birthday until he was eighteen he would have a card or letter from his mother.

'What's in the cards, Mum?' Leo asks, feeling one of them and trying to guess.

'Secrets,' Mum says, smiling a smile that made everything seem all right, even though it wasn't. 'You'll have to wait to find out, won't you?'

Leo peers back into the box and notices a small bag of seeds. When he fishes one out, he sees a handwritten white label stuck on the side of the bag. It is Mum's handwriting:

Chamomile Lawn (Flowering Type). *Anthemis nobilis*

'What's *Anthemis nobilis*, Mum?' he asks. Ever since he can remember, Mum had been growing flowers from seeds in little trays and patiently moving the seedlings into small pots and then bigger pots.

'*Anthemis nobilis*,' she says, with an impish smile, 'is the proper name for chamomile flowers. All plants have Latin names. You know that.'

'But why are they in my Memory Box?' Leo asks.

Mum gazes at him, her hooded eyes red and heavy, as if every ounce of her energy is keeping them from closing.

'When I'm gone . . . you know, Lion; when I am no longer here.' Mum's hand smoothes his hair. 'They will remind you of today.'

She takes the seed bag in her hand, her arm resting on the tartan rug.

'If you look after these seeds, you'll grow hundreds of plants and from them thousands. Leo, you can grow chamomile forever.'

Mum smiles at the thought and pats Leo's knee.

'Be a love and get me the chamomile flowers from the top drawer in the kitchen.'

Leo leaves the balcony with its sounds of summer and walks the few yards inside, this time to the small kitchen in Mum's room. He opens the top drawer of the worktop and quickly finds the dried chamomile heads, the yellow middles from the flowers, shorn of the white petals and the stalks.

He hears Mum shouting from the balcony, her voice just strong enough to be heard.

'And boil the kettle, will you, Lion? And then bring the white teapot out. There's something I want to teach you how to do . . .'

When Leo is back on the balcony, he drops a handful of dried chamomile into the pot.

Carefully Mum picks up the steaming kettle and

pours the boiling water into the pot. She uses a spoon to mix in the flowers.

'That's what you do with chamomile flowers,' she says, her smile returning. 'You make chamomile tea.'

Mum places a tea-strainer on to the cup and leans back in her chair, considering her words.

'Chamomile has been used since ancient times to calm people, to make them relax. I want you to remember that when you're older. You must remember how to make it, though. Never add sugar, never add milk. Have some honey in it, if you like – even let it cool and drink it cold.

'But first,' she adds, 'you have to do this . . .'

Mum lifts the white pot. Her hand shakes with the effort and the lid of the pot rattles in its setting.

'What are you doing?' Leo asks, concerned. He doesn't think he's seen her do this before.

'I'm showing the pot to the angels, Lion. You lift it up and –' she winks – 'you . . . show it to the angels . . .'

'To the angels?' Leo asks as Mum lowers the pot and fills her cup. 'Why to the angels?'

'Because without that it isn't Leo's tea,' Mum says with another wink.

'But how do you know angels exist? I mean, have you ever seen one?'

Mum considers the question as she nurses her tea, occasionally taking a sip.

'Just because you can't see something,' she breathes, 'doesn't mean it isn't there.'

She seems to brighten suddenly and sits up, pointing out to sea.

'Can you see the line between the sea and the sky?' she asks. 'Look carefully, Lion, really try your best.'

Leo narrows his eyes and looks towards the blue horizon.

White flecks are dotted here and there: yachts and boats. A trail of whiteness like the vapour-trail of a plane betrays a power-boat.

'The line . . . it's hard to see,' he says. 'The sea and the sky, they sort of just look the same.'

Mum laughs gently.

'You can't see it often. But it is there . . . It has to be. It's hidden in the dazzling, Leo. Sometimes it's hidden in the clouds . . . but look carefully. Concentrate.

'See how the light glitters on the sea. How the sun seems to just hang there today below that canopy of clouds.'

Leo looks out to sea.

'It's beautiful,' she whispers, 'isn't it? I've tried to paint that line so many times . . . Sometimes you think you can see it, but then it vanishes . . .'

'What does it look like?' Leo asks. 'When you do see it?'

She reaches out to Leo, tracing his cheek with the back of her hand.

'It's like a long, thin pencil line across the sky,' she says. 'Have a look, darling. Can you see it?'

Leo looks out to the horizon and tries to see. But he cannot.

'We have so little time left, you and I,' Mum says with softness. 'I want to tell you something that's important, something I want you to remember . . . I want you to remember this for the rest of your life.

'There are only two things that really matter, Lion – one of them is love and the other is faith.

'Faith is knowing the line exists even when you can't see it. It's knowing,' she adds softly, 'that everything's going to be all right.'

'But everything *isn't* going to be all right, is it, Mum?' he whispers. 'You're going to –'

Mum puts her finger to his lips to shush him.

'In the end, everything is always all right. Remember that. Even your dad, Leo. He'll be all right too.'

Leo grimaces.

'But he went away, Mum . . . Why do you care about him?'

For a moment Mum falls silent, her head turned away.

'Love never truly dies,' she whispers.

She turns to look at him again. 'You know your dad loves you very much, don't you, Leo?'

Mum reaches out and takes his hand.

'When you were born, your dad held you through the night. Did I ever tell you that? He wouldn't let go of you, you see. He said he couldn't believe you were real.'

Leo shrugs his shoulders.

'But –' he starts.

Mum hushes him again.

'One day, you'll understand. I promise you. When you're bigger.'

Leo looks at the box again, running his fingers over the bright coloured jewels, feeling their shapes and sharpness.

'Why are you showing me all this now?' he asks. 'Shouldn't everything in the box be, well, a sort of surprise?'

'Oh there *will* be surprises, Lion. You can count on that.'

'Will they be nice ones?'

'Yes, Lion, they will be nice ones.'

'Only . . .' Leo's voice weakens slightly, 'only most surprises seem to be bad ones, don't they, even when they seem good at first? Like when your hair grew back and I thought you'd got better. Like when you and Dad stopped fighting because you'd decided not to live together . . .'

Mum reaches out to wipe away Leo's tears.

'Maybe we all have our share of surprises stored up, Lion. Maybe you've had all your bad ones early.'

Mum looks at Leo, looks straight at him.

'Maybe you've only got the good ones left.'

Leo holds Mum's gaze. He likes the quiet times between them.

'Are you scared of dying, Mum?' he says, hearing his own words come out all matter-of-fact.

She picks up a chamomile flower and turns it in her hand.

'I know there's no reason to be scared . . .' Mum says gently.

'So you're not, then? Scared . . .?'

Mum pauses, still turning the chamomile slowly.

'I . . . I don't . . .' she falters, 'I . . . don't want to leave you, Leo. You must know that. But I'm so small and the illness . . . you know, the cancer . . . well, it's so very big . . . There are things that are much bigger than us . . .

'I know it makes no sense, Leo. But I think there is a reason for all this. I think one day we will understand. But perhaps not just yet.'

Leo snuggles into her, wrapping his arms around her, holding her frailness as tightly as he dares.

'I don't expect you to understand, darling. I can't expect you to because I'm not sure I do. But I want you to remember what I said about faith and about love. They're little leaps, those things. But they're so important . . .

'You'll learn about faith, my darling. As for love . . .' Mum's voice begins to fade. It's hard to hear it.

'I love you so much, Leo, so very much . . .'

Leo sleeps now amid the slants of roofs and the beating of the lighthouse out across the town.

He sleeps. His arms, his legs thrust out, starfish shaped. A lonely boy in a lonely bed.

Chapter 6
Four Thirty

When Leo woke, he felt the darkness crowding in around him, pressing in.

He'd drifted off to sleep. He knew that. But he could tell it was still the middle of the night, the time when normal kids were fast asleep.

At first he just dozed, half-awake, the pins and needles caused by sleeping all stuck out like a starfish numbing his arms and legs. He snapped them back close to his body, so that he was closed up again. They felt strange and heavy, like they weren't his limbs at all.

What had happened in the night came back to him, playing like a movie inside his head. He saw things frame by frame and shot by shot.

He remembered the noise on the stairs and the banging of the door against the bed. He remembered Dad's shouting, the redness of his face. Most of all, he remembered falling and the pain of hitting the bedpost.

When he reached his hand up to feel the back of his head, the pain shot through him. There was a wetness there he didn't like the feel of, all clammy and hot. It ached too, coming and going to the rhythm of his beating heart.

Leo began to sense too that something else had changed . . . something in the room.

He remembered the shattering of glass. The crystal frame around the photo.

Instinctively his hands felt for smashed-up glass.

But there wasn't any. Leo slowly moved his hand down his duvet cover where he figured there'd be at least one or two glass shards.

Even when he pushed his hand down the side of the bed and felt the carpet, expecting to find big lumps of crystal, there was nothing.

Leo knew why there was no glass. Dad had been back. He'd sneaked in and tidied up. It had happened again. Dad had shouted and yelled, thrown things and smashed things up. And then he had quietly cleaned everything away. Why did he do that? It was like he was instantly sorry. Like he did things he didn't really want to do.

A light flashed through the room. The lighthouse. The great glass was turning, blinking golden paths across the empty sea. The light glinted at him each time before it flashed, a familiar red, like the embers of a homely fire.

Leo blinked too. And rubbed his eyes. He was fully awake now. And he had work to do! He glanced at the clock radio. It was 4.30 a.m.

When he stood up, a fuzziness gripped him and there was a ringing in his ears. He felt strangely dizzy like all the blood had left his head. Quickly he sat back down and closed his eyes. Slowly it passed.

When he pushed open his bedroom door, he saw something that made his heart leap. The upstairs landing light was on.

Mum's room! Had Dad been inside in the night? Just for once, had he actually left the door unlocked?

Leo moved swiftly up the stairs, but when he reached the door he faltered.

He tried to remember the last time he had been in the room, in real life and not just in his imagination. He wasn't sure, not quite.

But he knew what was in there. He knew what was on the other side of the door. He could picture Mum's chamomile sideboard, her plants in rows, her books. He could even smell her smell.

He turned the knob.

The door was locked. As usual.

Leo turned and sadly trudged back down the stairs. When he got to Dad's room, he peered inside and saw the bed. It was empty, the covers neatly tucked in by Mrs York, Dad's housekeeper. It looked like a bed on show in a furniture shop, untouched and perfect.

She would be here later. Mrs York. She'd be here to clear things up and open up the surgery.

Leo padded down the stairs and as he did so the noise of the television, blaring too loud for the hour, came up to meet him. Canned laughter from an old comedy show.

Nearing the foot of the stairs, the smells of the night came floating up as well: fatty food, the stench of cigarettes, the dull, flat smell of booze.

He could always smell the booze. Its smell gnawed at the insides of his nose, raw and mean. It smelt of nothing and everything.

There was a mirror in the hall and as he passed he saw himself.

People always said he looked like Mum; they were always saying it. Sometimes people he hadn't seen for ages would tousle his hair and he'd notice their eyes were wet and teary.

He liked that. It was like he was the proof she had been here; she had existed. Sometimes he thought he was the *only* proof.

He stared at himself, registering Mum's brown eyes, her chestnut hair. Even his nose was like hers, small and like a button.

Then he saw the blood on his cheek. He must have

touched his face after feeling the throbbing at the back of his head.

Dad had really hurt him this time.

Where was Dad? Leo knew. He'd be where he always was at this time of night.

When he got into the sitting-room, he saw he was right. Dad was asleep on the sofa, his glasses askew on his face, his white shirt a mass of mixed-up stains from drink and food.

Leo picked the glasses from Dad's face. They were smudged and finger-marked, greasy. Carefully, Leo cleaned the lenses one at a time, using his pyjama sleeve to shine them up. When he had finished, he folded them up and placed them on the table.

He picked up the TV remote and muted the sound. The sudden silence somehow shrank the room. Dad stirred slightly, but didn't wake.

One of the take-away trays was full of butted-out cigarette ends stuffed into the congealed food.

The aluminium tray sat, buckled at its edges, its mushed contents of cold, spiced meat and cigarettes too much to bear.

For a moment Leo thought he might be sick, his palm moving instinctively towards his mouth.

Then it passed. He was used to the smell, used to everything.

He fetched a new black plastic bag from the kitchen and began to fill it up. Carefully, he lifted the aluminium trays into the bag and dropped them in. The one full of cigarette butts fell in clumsily, coating the sides with stinking debris.

Dad just didn't seem to care. He didn't care about himself and he didn't care about him. Just like he hadn't cared about Mum.

One by one, Leo gathered up the bottles, noticing each one, each brand name on the side. Dad had patterns. There'd always be a few beer bottles with the vodka, like he had to build up to the killer stuff.

One of the vodka bottles was still full. It stood in front of Dad's sleeping form like a sentinel. Still waiting to impart its chaos, like a bullet locked and loaded in a gun. Leo would clear that one away later.

In the kitchen he lined up the nightly haul of bottles on the sink. Seven. That was one more than the night before and two more than normal. It was a record.

With one hand he held his nose against the stench and with the other he lifted each bottle and poured away what was left. Then he put the cold tap on full tilt to take away the last vestiges of the smell.

When he had finished, he put the bottles in the same black bag he had been using, unlocked the kitchen door and went out into the cold night. Quietly, so as not to wake the neighbours, he found the wheelie-bins in their usual place and dumped the bag inside one. The bin's top snapped shut with a satisfying plop.

Back inside, he opened the drawer next to the sink and took out a pair of yellow plastic gloves and Mrs York's blue-and-white checked cloths. He pulled open another cupboard and grabbed hold of some spray polish.

He dampened one of the cloths and began to clean away the bottle marks on the low table. He sprayed the table with white polish and then rubbed it expertly away.

Dad moved in his sleep, letting out an ugly grunt. But Leo knew he wouldn't wake. Nothing much would wake him now.

When Leo had finished, he stood back and surveyed his handiwork. The sitting-room and the kitchen were now spotless, everything in its place.

He had done a good job. All he had to do now was get rid of the bottle on the table.

Mrs York would be here in just over an hour. He felt an overwhelming tiredness.

Exhausted, Leo went over to the sofa and climbed on to it next to Dad. His father, still asleep, was turned away from him, his knees pulled up into a ball, the way a child might sleep.

Where had the dad gone that played football with him before breakfast, still in their pyjamas? Where was the dad he loved but could hardly even remember?

He missed that dad.

Leo put his arms around his dad and closed his eyes to try to sleep. He gripped his father like a stricken sailor hangs on to flotsam in a storm, his only hope, his only chance.

Chapter 7

Just an Act

'Morning, Lionopolous.'

Leo woke with a start from deep and lovely sleep. It was morning and slowly he took in where he was; he was on the sofa.

Dad was dressed smartly as if this were a normal day, as if Leo had dreamed what had happened in the night.

Leo knew that he too had to act normal. It was always like this. It was time for the daily performance to begin.

'Lionopolous. You awake?' Dad said.

'What . . . what do you mean, "Lion . . op . . ol . . ."?'

Leo struggled to pronounce the word. He gazed around the room, checking for tidiness, and when his eyes came to rest on the low table he realized with horror that the full bottle had disappeared.

Dad'd grabbed it and hidden it for later.

'Lionopolous,' said Dad, his face smiley, all shaved

and neat. 'It's what I called you when we were in Greece – you remember, when we went to see the Gods . . .'

Greece? Leo thought. Gods? What was he talking about . . .?

Leo felt for the wound on the back of his head, checking his hand and seeing there were still faint traces of his blood. Just for a moment he had prayed it *had* all been a dream but there was too much pain to remind him it hadn't.

'You remember the Gods, don't you, Lionopolous?' Dad was saying. 'Me showing you the statues?' he continued, as if nothing had happened.

As if everything was all right.

'Surely you remember the Parthenon?' Dad went on.

Leo nodded. It had been the last holiday they had all gone on together, as if they were an ordinary family.

Only they hadn't been ordinary. When were they ever ordinary? Hardly ever. Thanks to Dad.

He didn't remember the Parthenon. Not really. He knew it was the famous old ruin overlooking Athens on the Acropolis. He remembered pictures of it. Remembered the postcards.

All he remembered of that holiday was sitting on a plane between Mum and Dad. He remembered being the thing that had kept them from arguing just for a while, a human barrier between them.

He remembered Dad putting on his smiley voice and asking for more drinks from the lady pushing the trolley. He remembered noticing how she flushed slightly, looking embarrassed, when Dad had asked for two 'spare bottles' which he had shoved in the pocket in front of him for later.

Maybe they *had* gone to the Parthenon. Or maybe they had just gone near it and bought the postcards for later. Leo had no idea but he knew he couldn't trust his dad to tell the truth.

Dad was always lying. He lied for no reason. He even lied about the small things.

He was lying now and he wasn't even speaking, because his whole rotten life was a lie. Outside in Easthampton everybody thought he was great. Good old reliable Dr Rake.

Inside the house Leo and Dad were actors in a play that played every day and every night. But they were the only audience too.

And yet it was always like this. Or it seemed to have been for as long as Leo could remember.

A normal dad would have asked Leo why he was on the sofa. A normal dad would have been horrified by the blood matted in his hair. But if he'd had a normal dad there wouldn't even be any blood. And he'd have slept right through the night too.

What about the mess and where it went? Dad

knew Leo had tidied up. It happened every single night. But Dad would pretend and Leo would pretend, so everything seemed normal when it wasn't.

Dad had gone to the bookshelves that lined the sitting-room wall. Dad loved history. Or he used to. He had hundreds of books. Books on medicine, of course, but books on Greece too. Books he never touched any more.

Leo studied him, noticing how well dressed he looked, wondering how long he could keep up the act.

'I wanted to show you . . .' Dad was saying, his back turned, straining up to reach a book on the top shelf, '. . . something rather special.'

When he turned round, the morning light streamed through the front window catching his glasses, which flashed in the glare, spotless and shiny. Leo remembered how he'd cleaned them on his pyjama sleeve.

Dad sat down on the sofa, crowding into Leo's space. He smelt like he did every morning: as if he'd tried to clean away the smells of the night before but hadn't quite pulled it off. He smelt of mints and aftershave, so strong it made Leo's nose itch inside.

'When I was about your age, I went to Greece for the first time,' he carried on, waving a narrow book. 'This was my Baedekers, my guidebook.'

Dad paused, scrunching up his face as if something was causing him pain.

'I guess Mrs York will be here in a jiffy,' he said. 'I'll tell you what, though – I'm not feeling a hundred per cent. Thinking about it . . . I might get Mrs York to close up the surgery today. She'll be here in a minute, won't she . . .?'

He watched Dad's eyes, how they darted nervously from thing to thing, always moving, never settling; and never – for as long as Leo could remember – ever looking him straight in the eye.

There was a noise at the door, a key placed in a familiar lock.

A shrill cry from the hall.

'H-e-l-l-o-o – i-t-s – m-e-e-e-e . . .!'

This was Mrs York, come to clean, come to scrub, come to help pretend.

Leo hated her. He hated her because she was a walk-on part in the daily drama that was his life. She pretended just like Dad did, just like he himself did.

Only she was worse. Much worse. Because she didn't *need* to pretend.

Leo knew what was coming next. He knew everybody else's lines as well as his own.

'Oooh, I must say,' Mrs York cooed, 'this place is spick and span. I swear it gets tidier every day.'

She looked at Leo.

'That's a nasty mark on the back of your head,' she said. 'How did you do that to yourself, young man?'

It was Dad's turn to say his lines and he had them down to perfection.

'Oh, you know what boys are like . . .' he rushed, glancing in Leo's general direction.

Leo looked at the floor and then at Mrs York who had folded her arms, expectant.

Dad changed the subject.

'Do you know, Mrs Y, I'm not exactly feeling myself today. I'm just not a hundred per cent . . .'

'Oh, Dr R,' she cooed again, 'I wonder if you shouldn't close up the surgery, you know. You do look a bit peaky.'

And so it went on. So it always went on.

The cut in Leo's head still throbbed. He'd have to pat it clean before he left.

He'd slip away, as he always did, almost unnoticed. He'd pull on his school clothes, hoping they were clean, pick up any sports kit that happened to be washed and make his way down Pier Road to school.

He scanned the room for his bag. He couldn't see it anywhere.

Where was it? Then he noticed it, pushed up against the sofa, round the side.

'Right . . . I'm off to school,' he mumbled to nobody in particular.

He left them agreeing to cancel the surgery and ring the patients one by one.

'Just get some rest,' he heard Mrs York saying. 'I say, you really do look a bit under par . . .'

It was chilly outside when Leo eventually left, and he buttoned up his coat as he walked down the path and through the tiny gate.

Something made Leo look back at the house. He saw Dad in his bedroom window. He was smoking. Smoking yet again. Then he closed the curtains, like the curtains at the end of a play.

The performance was over for another day.

Chapter 8
A Sleepless PM

Barnaby Green wasn't sure what being Prime Minister was supposed to feel like but he was pretty sure it wasn't like this.

He felt so tired all the time. And powerless. Like he was in charge of a giant super-computer that was supposed to control everything but wasn't plugged in.

And yet he was the Prime Minister. He was the Prime Minister of Great Britain and Northern Ireland, and he had been now for nearly one whole year.

Barnaby sat at the desk in his office, hidden at the back of 10 Downing Street. His computer screen booted up and flickered into life, while Barnaby doodled on a pad.

He wrote:

Why can't I get anything done? Is it because a) I am a rubbish PM, b) all PMs are rubbish, c) nobody listens to what I say . . .

He paused for a moment, smiling to himself, imagining what would happen if the newspapers somehow got hold of his doodles, then added:

Or do I haven't got the courage of my convictions.

Barnaby tore off the piece of paper and held it up in the dim light, leaning back in his chair, re-reading his own words. Then, his lips pursed, he crushed the sheet into a tiny ball and lobbed it into the air. It landed back on his desk, where it rolled towards him.

His computer broke the night's silence, suddenly exploding into a musical greeting played too loud for the hour.

The silence returned.

The door creaked and for a second Barnaby's heart plummeted like a stone. He thought it was Claudia, his secretary. Maybe she had come to work early? Maybe there was a war on? Maybe he was the last to know?

But it wasn't Claudia. It was Bobby, otherwise known as the Bobster, also known as the Downing Street moggie or the First Cat.

Bobby had become famous since Barnaby had taken over as Prime Minister. Whenever Bobby went outside the famous black door of Number 10, the ever-present cameras whirred almost as much as when the PM did.

'Hello, Bobster,' Barnaby soothed as the big fat tabby cat jumped surprisingly lightly on to his Prime Ministerial desk.

Barnaby stroked him and Bobby pushed his big furry head into Barnaby's hand like cats do, all heavy and warm.

'You understand me, don't you, Bobster,' Barnaby purred. 'You don't care who I am, do you, Bob? And you can do something I seem to have forgotten how to do . . . s-l-e-e-p . . .'

Absent-mindedly, Barnaby went into his spam folder and scrolled down the black unread emails.

Something caught his eye. Something written in bold, in the message header field:

RE: PLEASE OPEN PIER ROAD SCHOOL LIBRARY

Pier Road School! That was *his* old school!

Memories began to flood into his mind. Memories of the first day of school, of being walked down Pier Road by his mum and not wanting to hold her hand. Wanting to walk on his own, all grown up.

How he missed his mum. She'd died before he'd become Prime Minister. She'd be proud of him. He knew that. But she would never know.

He began to read the email.

From: leo200@mac.com
To: primeminister@gsi.no10.gov.uk
Dear Prime Minister,
I don't know if you'll get this but I hope you do
because Manders, that's my teacher, well he
thinks I posted the letter to you, the one about
the library but Dad spilled his drink on it and I had
to throw it away. I won't tell Manders that of
course. I mean I can't. I'll just say I lost it, kind of.
Well, you don't need to know it all!

I'm typing this really fast. Mum taught me. I
can type faster than I can write if you want to
know the truth.

Anyway, Manders told our class you used to
be a pupil at our school. He says he taught you
and all. He says we should all be proud because
the Prime Minister went to our school. It was my
idea to ask you, though.

Sorry. I haven't explained. You see I don't get
to sleep very much so I'm really tired. I can't
sleep because my dad is always up. Only nobody
knows. I can't tell anyone.

You don't count as telling as a) you're the
Prime Minister and won't care about my
problems, and b) because there's no way you'll
get this email anyway!

I got the general details by going to the website they have for 10 Downing Street. Then I guessed your own email. But I bet I got it wrong. It's too obvious. Manders says I never get anything right.

Manders said we've never had a library. He says you'll remember all the shelves along the corridor.

Mind you, he says it didn't stop you working. He says you read and read, says you never stopped.

Not like us lot, he says. Not like the new lot. We're useless, he says.

Anyway. They've built a brand-new library, you see. It's nearly finished now.

I thought it would be good if you came back and opened it. Back to Easthampton.

If you want to come, can you ring us up? The school is on Easthampton 676063. Mrs Turner is the head. She's OK. She's better than Manders.

From Leo Rake, Class 5M, aged ten

P.S. Manders said you and your mum used to live up near the water tower. But then she went and died. My mum went and died as well. This is a picture I scanned in to show you what she looked like. It used to be up on the hall wall, but Dad took it down. I really miss her.

The PM downloaded the attachment and the picture of three faces slowly began to fill up his screen: this boy Leo and his dad and his mum.

They looked so happy, he thought. There was something about the email that had brought back memories, though, something that gnawed at him, that wouldn't go away.

Then he remembered what it was. It was that name, that teacher's name. Manders!

Somewhere inside the Prime Minister's memory an image of a young teacher shouting at him came to the fore. He remembered something the teacher had said to him once in class.

'You'll never amount to much, Barnaby Green.'

He could see him now, standing at the front of the class.

The Prime Minister pictured Manders. He would have been fresh out of college, a new teacher. He remembered the fuzz on his face, like he was trying to grow a beard but was still too young.

Then he paused. He wasn't supposed to send emails without Claudia showing them to all kinds of people. He wasn't allowed to communicate with anybody any more. He smiled, remembering how he had discussed the very thing with the American President when he'd visited him in Washington.

'They tried to take my Blackberry away from me,' he had told him. 'But I'm keeping it and that's for sure. I need to keep in contact with normal people!'

The Prime Minister made a decision and began to tip-tap his reply to Leo, still unsure if he would actually send it. After all, he thought, he *was* the Prime Minister and Prime Ministers didn't normally email schoolboys, even if they did have a few things in common.

And they did have a lot in common, Barnaby began to think.

His thoughts turned from Manders to his own mum. He thought about Leo and the lady in the picture with the brown eyes. She looked just like her son, he thought.

Then he continued to type:

From: primeminister@gsi.no10.gov.uk
To: leo200@mac.com
Dear Leo,
I miss my mum too. It isn't fair, is it, when your mum dies? There's always so much you wish you'd said.

I'm lucky compared to you, though. I was grown up when my mum died. It's just that she never got to see what I became, that's all.

I'm looking at your photo. Your mum looks very beautiful and lovely, Leo. It's a great photo.

Of course I'll come and open your library. I'll give your Mrs Turner a ring.

I do remember Mr Manders, by the way. I don't think I'll ever forget him. He had just started out teaching when I was there. He wasn't very nice to me, Leo. He wasn't nice at all.

I remember he was always trying to grow a beard. Has he got one by now?

Shall we come up with a plan for him, you and me? Let me have a Prime Ministerial think . . . sounds like we both owe Mr Manders!

I'm putting my thinking cap on.

Barnaby

The Prime Minister looked at the email on his screen and had some second thoughts. Should he really send it? For a moment his finger hovered over the Delete button.

Then he clicked on Send and turned off the computer.

Chapter 9

Disaster!

Leo was late for school. He was always late for school. In fact, if he ever turned up on time he reckoned Manders would be lost for words.

He knew what would happen when he arrived in the classroom. It was the same every day, but today it would be worse. Today Manders would just carry on from yesterday.

Leo would try to block all of them out as usual. Put the world on mute. He'd try to be there in the England locker room before the big game. There with the lads. Rio and Shauny. Rooney and JT.

But even that might not work. When he'd been younger, Leo could disappear inside his head for hours, even a whole day. He'd play game after game, see England through the qualifiers and into the final stages. Squeak a win against France in the semis – after extra time – maybe even on penalties.

And then the final . . .

Only what was happening in the real world was

getting worse. He couldn't keep it out as easily as he used to.

Like the things Manders had said about him being stupid. Maybe he was right. Maybe he *was* an idiot.

After all, emailing the Prime Minister! As if! How could he think a powerful man like that would bother to read something from a muppet like him, even if by some miracle he had got the right address?

They would already be in class. They would already have sat down. The register would have been called and when it had got to Rake they'd all have had a good laugh.

Leo hitched up his bag, which felt heavy across his shoulders. When he reached the school, he stuck his head down and walked across the playground to the classroom, keeping his eyes on the mish-mash of crossed white lines and curves denoting this sport and that.

He was in the middle of the playground when he heard the first jeer through the open window. He'd been spotted.

'Leo Rake's here, Sir!' Mary Chesterton had shouted. He heard the laughter, then Manders's voice, hushing them all down.

As he walked into the classroom, struggling to take off his heavy bag and get to his desk, he mumbled, 'Sorry I'm late, Sir . . .'

'Ah! Mr Rake has graced us with an appearance.

He says he's sorry. Well, we're all sorry, aren't we.'

Manders was performing once again, his hands stuck on his hips and his head thrown back.

'Mr Rake likes to pop in here occasionally,' he said, as if addressing an entirely new audience unfamiliar with the characters on the stage, 'when he can fit us into his busy social diary.'

Leo sat down at his desk, trying to pull his bag's strap over his head. He fixed his gaze on the head of the boy in front of him and tried to disappear. But he could see the boy's shoulders were shaking with laughter. They were all laughing.

'Tell us, Mr Rake, have you had a reply to your email from the Prime Minister or did he call you directly on his home phone to invite you to tea with the Queen and her corgis?'

Leo ignored the laughter. For a moment he thought about the email and wondered if he should have checked his computer. But he was sure it would have been a waste of time.

'What's our excuse for being late today, then?' Manders demanded, really hitting his stride now, walking between desks to reach his prey. 'Breakfast with the Prime Minister? Did Rake partake of some bacon sandwiches with his new bosom buddy, Mr Green?' Manders sneered.

'No, Sir,' Leo said, his eyes searching for Flora and finding her at her new desk way off at the front.

'You're mumbling, boy. Don't mumble. I don't like mumbling,' Manders barked.

Leo was angry now. He felt the hotness building up inside him, filling him up. His mind was fizzing. He felt clammy and sweaty and all closed in.

He slumped into his chair, watching as Manders got nearer.

When he reached Leo, he leant down towards him, like he was looking at something on a market stall and deciding whether to buy.

'Isn't Mr Rake going to take his bag off his shoulders?' he said. 'After all, you may as well stay for what little of the lesson still remains . . .'

Leo finally moved the strap over his head and just for a moment the bag hung free. Then he held it as high as he could and let it drop.

THUMP! It landed with a louder noise than he expected.

The class hushed. Heads turned, looking first at Leo and then at Manders.

'Your bag's blocking the aisle. Move it,' Manders said.

Leo glanced at his bag. It slouched on the floor, then, as if in slow motion, it slowly slumped over. It gaped open, its contents disturbed by the fall and spilling out.

The class watched as Manders slowly returned to the front of the class, talking as he went, as if nothing had happened.

The first Leo knew of the vodka bottle was the loud rolling sound of glass on the classroom's hard wooden floor.

In absolute horror, Leo looked down and saw the bottle with VLADIVOSTI! on the side slowly rolling down the aisle towards the front of the class.

Then he realized. Dad! That was where he'd hidden the bottle. He'd gone and put it in Leo's school bag!

The bottle seemed to be picking up speed as it rolled. Manders was writing on the whiteboard, his back turned to the class. But as the bottle rolled, more and more heads turned.

It was rolling towards Manders!

Kids were nudging each other; a murmur started which grew into a loud chatter.

'QUIET!' Manders bellowed. But still his back was turned as he finished writing on the board.

Leo sat paralysed, replaying in his head what must have happened, picturing Dad pushing the bottle into his bag.

It was too late to stand up and snatch it. There was nothing he *could* do.

'Since you are so keen to talk this morning, perhaps somebody can tell me the name of the author who wrote these fine words I am writing on the board?' Manders was saying, his back still turned.

The bottle stopped rolling, and came to a halt right

behind Manders, right next to the seat Flora had been moved to.

As the teacher turned round, Leo awaited his fate. He felt like his world was ending. He would have to explain where the bottle had come from. Things would never be the same again.

Then something extraordinary happened.

Flora picked up the bottle. Leo watched mesmerized as she calmly bent down from her desk, grasped the bottle and put it in her own bag on the floor.

Leo couldn't believe what he was seeing. Flora turned, briefly, and – for a split second – their eyes met.

Had she got away with it? The class had quietened and Leo felt as if the whole thing had been a dream. Maybe nobody had noticed?

But Manders had noticed.

'What's that in your bag, young lady?' he demanded, standing in front of Flora's desk.

Leo's heart dropped. There was a steeliness in Manders's eyes Leo couldn't remember seeing before.

Manders stood before Flora, the murmuring in the classroom mounting once again. A girl whispered, 'It's a bottle, Sir.' A few laughed and then the Kerry girl said in a louder voice, 'She's been at the drink, Mr Manders!'

'Silence!' Manders bellowed. He turned back to

Flora. 'Open your bag, please. Now!'

The class was still and silent, full of poisoned expectation.

'I SAID: OPEN YOUR BAG!'

Manders was shouting in her face.

'COME ON, YOUNG LADY! OPEN UP!'

Flora had begun to sob, her cries the only sound in the hushed class.

It was too much for Leo. Flora had always seemed so grown up to him, so in charge. But now she just looked like a little girl being bullied.

He stood up and heard himself shouting, almost as if he was somebody else.

'Leave her alone! Leave her alone!'

And then he was running as fast as he could to the front of the class. With all the strength he could summon, he pushed Manders away from Flora.

The teacher fell, crashing against the whiteboard. As he fell, Manders did not say a thing – his face a snapshot of shock, his features frozen by surprise.

Then Leo was shouting again and he was waving the bottle in the air like a trophy.

'It's mine, Mr Manders, it's mine. It's *my* bottle – it rolled out of *my* bag. She only picked it up. Are you happy now? Are you *happy* now?'

Leo stood totally still, the bottle above his head, breathing hard, his energy spent.

The classroom door was open.

Disaster!

Mrs Turner stood surveying the scene from the doorway. Leo had no idea how long she had been there.

'Leo Rake and Flora Long,' she said. 'My office. *Immediately.*'

Chapter 10
Flora's Secret

'Sit down, both of you,' Mrs Turner said as Leo and Flora entered her office, pointing to two seats in front of her desk. 'I will be back in two minutes.'

The headmistress closed the door and stood just beyond it in the small ante-room where Mrs Bedford, the school secretary, had her desk. Leo could see them silhouetted in the dappled glass of the door.

There was birdsong outside the office and the dripping of a tap from a small sink in the corner. Leo and Flora sat in silence, side by side.

Mrs Turner's wall clock tick-tocked and dust seemed to rise from lines of higgledy old books on the bookshelves. And still the dripping of the tap.

It was Flora who broke the silence as she turned to Leo and said simply: 'Leo . . . Thanks.'

'It's me that should be thanking you,' said Leo. He checked the door and kept his voice low. 'You were very brave.'

Flora leant her head closer to Leo's, making sure she couldn't be heard by anyone but him.

'Old Manders,' she smiled. 'You floored him!'

Her smile disappeared and she grew more serious.

'That bottle,' she whispered. 'It's your dad's, isn't it?'

Leo didn't say anything. He was watching the way Mrs Turner was talking to Mrs Bedford. The way her hands were doing the talking, telling her to do something. He watched as the secretary's distorted image picked up the telephone and began to speak.

It wasn't that he hadn't heard Flora. It was just that he didn't know what to say. After all, he'd kept his secrets for such a long time.

But Flora wasn't giving up, not by a long chalk.

'It's your dad's bottle, isn't it? Did he hide it there? Maybe he forgot where he'd put it . . . Leo . . . I know . . . I know how it is.'

Leo saw something in Flora's gaze and knew she understood.

'Has it got something to do with why you're always late?' she continued. 'You're always so tired, but you never say why. Is it because you *can't* tell anybody?

'Not even me.'

Leo gazed at Flora in astonishment, wondering how she seemed to be reading his mind.

'How come you know . . . I mean how can you . . .?' he said.

Flora had reached over and put her hand on his forearm, squeezing gently.

'It happened to me,' she whispered. 'Before I came here, before Mum left. I know what it's like . . . Nobody talks about it; it's the biggest secret –'

There was a noise at the door and the two stood up. Flora pulled her arm away.

Mrs Turner came back in. Leo expected to be shouted at, and prepared for the onslaught.

But Mrs Turner didn't sit behind her desk. Instead she moved her chair and sat down right in front of them.

'There's no need to stand, you two,' she said in a voice that sounded unexpectedly kind.

As they both sat down again, Mrs Turner leant towards them, trying to be friendly, her head lower than theirs so she looked upwards at them, like a football coach at a half-time team talk.

'I want to tell you something straight away and make it very clear,' she said, speaking slower than she normally did. 'I am not angry with you. Neither of you is in trouble. Do you understand?'

'But Mr Manders –' Leo started. Mrs Turner interrupted him.

'Never mind Mr Manders for now. What you did, Leo, the way you behaved was unacceptable and we will have to come back to that. But . . .'

Mrs Turner smiled, her voice softening even more.

'. . . I want to talk about that bottle. I want you to tell me whose it was. I want you to tell me how it got into Mr Manders's classroom.'

Neither spoke. The tap dripped on.

'All right,' said Mrs Turner after a while. 'Leo. I don't want you to be frightened. I want you to know I am trying to help. Mr Manders tells me you've been late for school even more lately. I know you are a clever boy. I just need to find out what's been going on.'

She paused.

'I know it's been hard for you, Leo, since your mum died. It's just you and Dad at home, isn't it?'

That was a mean trick, Leo thought. Why did she have to start talking about Mum?

Leo wanted to be back in his world. He shut his eyes and summoned up the green of Wembley's pitch, the ball lobbed by Rooney into his path . . .

But it was no good. The here and now was pulling him back. The world would not go on mute this time.

He could feel Flora swallow hard next to him.

'Leo. I want to ask you about your dad. He drinks alcohol, doesn't he? I imagine he may drink a very great deal. Is that the case, Leo? Do you want to talk about it?'

Leo felt cramped and crowded. He was sweating.

Mrs Turner was still waiting for an answer, but

when Leo opened his mouth something strange happened. He could hear the words in his head but he just couldn't say them out loud.

And then Flora spoke, filling the silence once again.

'Are you asking what happens when mums and dads drink?' she said, her voice raised like she was angry. 'Is that what you're asking, Miss? Cos if it is, *I* can tell you, Miss. I can tell you everything . . .'

Mrs Turner looked from Leo to Flora, her eyes growing wider, trying to work things out. 'You, Flora?'

Flora was breathing faster now, like she was getting ready to run a race. Like she was getting ready for something big.

'Oh I can tell you what *happens* all right, Miss,' she said, her voice deeper than usual, her emotions barely checked. 'They make promises about all sorts of things and then forget. They shout and rave and then forget. They say they hate you, they say they love you and it's all just lies because all they love, all they *really* love, is the stuff in the bottles!'

Flora began to cry, great fat tears rolling down her face.

'And then they fall asleep and you have to cover up. Lie and pretend, just like they do . . .' she continued.

Mrs Turner tried to comfort Flora.

'Does this happen a lot?' she asked, offering her a paper hankie.

'Not any more. Not to me. It used to. Then Mum went away and I moved here to live with Dad.' She sniffed before blowing her nose.

'I know it's just you and Dad,' the headmistress said, 'but I didn't know that –'

'Well, you wouldn't, would you?' Flora snapped. 'Because everybody covers up. Even my dad. It's one of these things nobody talks about even though it's everywhere.'

Leo sat in stunned silence, wondering how it was possible his friend's life was so like his.

Mrs Turner had turned to him again.

'It's been really tough for you, hasn't it, Leo? How long, Leo? How long have you been covering up for your dad?'

Leo could only whisper.

'Since before Mum died . . .'

He could no longer hold Mrs Turner's gaze. This was the end, he thought, the end of everything.

'Are you scared of your dad?' Mrs Turner asked, her voice calm and slow. 'Does he . . . does he hurt you sometimes?'

Leo could feel his face going red. He remembered the cut on the back of his head. Instinctively he lifted his hand towards the wound and then just as quickly put it down.

'No, Miss,' he said quickly.

She was in front of him now, her face level with his.

'What's it like, Leo? What's it like when your dad gets drunk? Would it be better . . . I mean, would you like it if you could go elsewhere? I mean not live with your dad at all? Would that be good?'

Leo didn't know what to do or say. He was paralysed with the fear of what might happen. But he knew he had to answer; he had no choice.

'I don't want to have to move,' he said.

'But it happens all the time. Doesn't it?' she was asking. 'Dad and the drink.'

Leo felt like his whole world was crashing in. Everything he knew might be taken away and replaced with . . . *what*?

'What happens now, Miss?' he whispered. 'Now that you know.'

Mrs Turner glanced at the outer office. The figure of Mrs Bedford reminded Leo of her phone call. Somebody had been called; something was bound to happen. Then two words popped uninvited into his mind.

Social services!

The call Mrs Bedford had made would have been to them. They would arrive soon and take him away. Away from the house. Away from Mum's room and the Memory Box.

It was what he had fought so long to avoid.

Mrs Turner had begun to talk. To answer his question.

But he knew he mustn't listen, mustn't be persuaded. Instead they had to get away.

He and Flora had to *escape*.

Mrs Turner was still speaking. She kept talking about 'options'. He didn't know what she meant.

There was *this* option and there was the *other* option. But he didn't like the sound of either. More to the point, when he caught Flora's eye he could see she didn't either.

He could see she was thinking the same thing. She wanted to get out too.

Suddenly Leo stood up, grabbing hold of Flora's arm.

He yanked open the dappled-glass door and they darted through Mrs Bedford's office, the secretary's face a picture of shock, her mouth wide open.

Then they were out, through her office and down the corridor.

Mrs Turner was shouting, her voice behind them growing fainter as they ran.

'Flora! Leo! Come back here! Come back . . .'

'Where are we going?' Flora asked breathlessly as they reached the playground, trying to keep up. 'What's this all about?'

'Just keep running,' Leo urged. 'Don't you see?

This is my last chance . . . They'll always be asking questions now. They'll never ever stop.'

Then they were out of school and they were running. They made it across the netball pitches and out of the gate, but still they did not stop.

Chapter 11
Faith Not Sight

By the time they reached the bus stop Leo's mind was racing. He'd begun to hatch a plan.

He knew he was right. Now that Mrs Turner knew about Dad, things had changed forever. The social services people would be on their trail. Right now. There'd be questions to answer. They needed time to work out what they were going to do and what they were going to say.

They'd go to the cemetery, he decided. He knew it was a funny place to hide away, but he liked to visit Mum as often as he could, go and see where she was buried. It was their special place to be together.

In any case, no one would think to look for them there.

They waited for the number 601, the bus he always got on to go to see Mum.

Later, as it stopped and started through the town, he and Flora fell into a comfortable silence, the way friends do.

97

They sat together on the front row of the double-decker's top deck; behind them rows and rows of empty seats.

Leo looked out of the window at Easthampton's neat roads moving in front of them, like a movie playing on a giant screen.

He took in the noises of the journey: the ping of the bell before stops, the shuddering of the bus, the muttered greetings to the driver and the chink of change into the bowl.

Soon the buildings grew sparser and, as Leo looked back, the lighthouse seemed tiny as it receded into the distance. Then hard brown fields reclaimed the landscape, littered with great corrugated pig sheds.

They passed a half-ruined church with crumbled edges.

Still they hadn't spoken. Each alone with their thoughts.

Leo wondered what Flora was thinking. He wondered what things were like for her at home, living just with her dad.

How many other kids had the same secret as they did? How many mums? How many dads?

And what would happen now? He wondered what social services people were like and what they did exactly. Did they still have children's homes?

Eventually Flora broke the quietness.

'This is a special journey for you, isn't it?' she said.

'Going to the cemetery. Do you come on this bus to see her a lot?'

Leo nodded.

'You're the first person I've brought,' he said.

'Is it . . . is it the only way of remembering . . .?' Flora asked, the bus juddering as it pulled away from another bus stop.

'I have the Memory Box too,' Leo replied. 'Or I will have one day.'

'Memory Box?' Flora asked, looking quizzical. 'What's a Memory Box?'

Leo began to explain.

'We made it together, me and Mum. Ages ago really. We painted it all up and put a picture of us on the top. We put jewels on it too. Well, not jewels exactly, more those glass shiny things you get in the craft shop – do you know the one I mean? The one in the High Street. Opposite the Post Office.'

Flora smiled. Leo carried on. It was good to talk about the Memory Box with someone else.

'She put things in it. Like some of her paintings. Her diaries. And she wrote me cards and letters for my birthdays –'

'You mean like birthday cards all stored up?' Flora said. 'That must be so lovely for you, though, knowing you're going to get one every year from her.'

Leo's face crumpled.

'I'm not sure what they are, really – cards or letters.

Maybe I've got both. You see, I haven't had one. I mean I haven't been able to . . .

'You see, the box is in Mum's room, at the top of the house. And I'm not allowed in. I haven't been in since she died.'

Flora turned to him, her face a picture of concern, her eyes wide. 'But why not?'

'I'm not allowed, that's all,' Leo said flatly. 'It's always locked. The room. Dad used to say I was too young to go there, that it might upset me. As if, as if . . . I could be upset any more than I am.'

Flora's voice was raised now. She seemed cross and worked-up.

'And what does your dad say now?'

'Nothing,' shrugged Leo. 'We never mention it. It's like we've done some secret deal . . . Only we haven't . . . not really. If I bring it up, I know he'll get angry and then I'll never see it.'

They passed a sign at the side of the road: *Easthampton Cemetery ¼ mile.*

Leo tapped Flora's arm.

'Next stop,' he said. 'Look, it's just up here . . .'

They walked alongside a tall red-brick wall that curved gently away from them, as if inviting them to follow, guiding them in. Eventually the wall brought them to a wrought-iron gate.

'This is it. The cemetery,' Leo whispered, watching

Flora peering through the black-painted bars into the private world beyond.

Leo pushed the gate. Despite its great size and weight it opened easily.

It was warmer now and the sky was a faultless blue, the spring sun casting shafts across the rows of headstones.

'It's beautiful,' Flora said, looking around at the neatness. 'Look at all those flowers everywhere. I know it sounds weird, but I've never seen such a beautiful place.'

She knelt down and ran her hand along a grass border, so straight, so perfect. She looked up at Leo, the sunlight catching her hair. She was smiling.

'It's like every single inch of the cemetery is special,' she said. 'Every bit is cared for. Every bit is loved. It's a precious place, this, isn't it?'

It made Leo feel happy she understood. But somehow he knew he didn't need to say anything. Here things could go unsaid.

It was a place of whispered truths. Where Leo would see people with sad faces kneeling to speak to mums or dads, sons or daughters. Yet it was a place of unexpected happiness and hope. A place he had grown to love.

They walked together down a path between the graves. They passed a new grave, still just a wooden cross with a metal sign on where the pieces met. The sign had a name on it. Leo remembered being told how the site needs to settle before the headstone is put on. He remembered how he'd hated leaving Mum with just a wooden cross.

'Can I ask you something about your mum?' Flora said. 'When she was alive. Did she ever talk about your dad and – you know – the drinking?'

Leo tried to remember, running memories through his mind.

'I don't think so, no. But they split up, you see. Dad said he wanted to go travelling and he left us in the house. Even the surgery closed . . . until after Mum died and he moved back in with me.'

Flora nodded.

'Same here,' she said. 'My mum and dad split up too. They never talked about it, though. They just pretended it wasn't happening.'

Leo knew exactly what Flora meant because it had happened to him. For the first time ever he had somebody to talk to. Somebody who understood.

'It's like my nan,' he said. 'She's my dad's mum, right. I think she knows about Dad but she never does anything to help me. Once I did try to tell her and she just hushed me up. It's like she doesn't *want* to know.

'I can't work out why he doesn't just pack it in. I mean, why keep on drinking that stuff if it turns you into an idiot and . . . well . . . makes everything bad?

'Sometimes I see the old dad. I can – I can kind of see him in there . . . do you know what I mean? I don't know how to describe it. I thought about it the other day. It's like he's in there but he can't get out.'

Flora was nodding.

'Your dad sounds just like my mum,' she said, blowing out all her breath and pursing her lips. 'When she drank, she changed. It was like Dr Jekyll and Mr Hyde – you know, in the story, where the same person can be really nasty or really nice –'

'And you never know which one you're going to get,' Leo said, smiling in recognition.

'When Dad wakes up in the morning, we pretend,' Leo carried on. 'I tidy everything up in the night. Sometimes even he tidies up his mess too. Then when we get up we carry on like it's all normal.'

Flora smiled. 'Do you know what? I used to *like* the smell of the drink on Mum's breath – I mean at first, before things got worse . . .'

Leo noticed Flora had reddened slightly, as if she was embarrassed.

'When she drank, she'd give in easily. She'd let me have what I wanted. I used to wait for the sound of the cork popping – you know, that plonky sound. Then I'd ask for extra pocket money and she'd say yes. Then later when she fell asleep I'd wish I hadn't. I'd feel guilty, feel like it was my fault.'

'Your fault?' Leo said. 'How could it be *your* fault?'

'I don't know,' Flora said quietly. 'I know it's not my fault but . . . it's the way it makes me feel inside. Like, if I was a better daughter maybe she wouldn't drink so much? Do you know what I mean, Leo?'

What Flora said made sense to Leo. It made him feel better, like somehow he was not the only one.

He was going to reply but instead he looked down at the headstones, reading off names that had become familiar to him.

In Loving Memory
Donald Hector McIntosh
Aged 77
Husband Father Grandfather
Beloved by All

Then another:

Here Lies
Joyce Mary Varley
1926–1981

'My mum's just up here,' Leo said, pointing up ahead of them.

They walked in silence for another minute or so and then, through the breeze, there was a sound rather like the tinkling of the high notes on a piano. A glassy chiming in the gentle wind.

'What's that noise?' Flora asked.

'Wind chimes,' Leo explained. 'They're wind chimes. I hang them up in the tree, on the branches above Mum's grave.'

They had arrived at the grave now.

'They're beautiful,' Flora said. 'It's like she's never alone.'

Leo looked up at the chimes.

'There's loads of them here now. In other trees – you see? Other people have done the same thing as me . . . You can hear them all over.'

Leo's voice was low now, like he was speaking to himself.

'I'm going to get some more and hang them in the garden,' he whispered.

But Flora had heard. She was standing right next to him now.

'So you can remember,' she said, smiling.

Mum's gravestone was a lighter granite than most of the others, a kind of speckled white and grey. And it was narrower. But it was taller too, and on it in large, proud letters read the words:

> *Sarah Rake*
> *1972–2008*
> *'We walk by faith,*
> *not by sight'*

'What does it mean? "We walk by faith, not by sight"?' Flora asked.

'It's something she said I should remember,' Leo said, wondering why on earth he hadn't thought about the words properly before. 'She said just because you can't see something doesn't mean it isn't there . . .

'She was always going on about the line between the sea and sky. She used to say you can hardly ever see it because of the dazzling.'

'The dazzling?' Flora asked. 'What's the dazzling?'

'It's the light on the horizon . . . the way it –' Leo tried to remember one of the words Mum always used to use – 'the way it shimmers . . .'

Flora was nodding, her face turned to his, a smile playing on her lips like she really understood.

'I know just what she meant. The glare from the sun.'

'She was always trying to paint it,' Leo said, 'but she said she hardly ever saw it. You know, the clouds or other things . . . getting in the way . . .'

Flora was silent for a moment, the only noise the tinkle of the chimes.

'But she did see it, though, every now and again?'

Leo tried to remember.

'I think she did,' he said.

'What about you?' Flora continued. 'Did you ever see it?'

It was late afternoon now. Time had passed so quickly. A breeze had caught the wind chimes, their glassy echo louder now.

'No . . .' Leo said softly, 'I never saw it.'

'I bet you will,' Flora said. 'One day.'

Leo wanted Flora to be right. But inside he knew she was wrong. He knew he'd never see the line.

Sometimes the things you wished for just never happened.

Chapter 12
Where Did All the Mums Go?

When they got to the bus stop, only a minute or two before the bus itself, Leo fumbled in his pocket for enough money for the bus fare home, but he only had enough money for one ticket.

'I'll walk home,' Leo said quickly, handing Flora the money from his pockets, knowing the bus might go in a flash and leave both of them stranded, not just him. 'Don't worry. It's not far.'

'But . . . you can't walk on your own,' Flora said, her eyes alert and worried-looking. 'It'll get dark soon.'

But Leo had made his mind up.

'Just get on,' he insisted. 'I'll be all right, honest. I often walk. You can always ring me at home maybe? We'll see each other tomorrow.'

As he said the word *tomorrow* he felt a heaviness inside. He had no idea what tomorrow would bring. Even the word was enough to fill him with dread.

'Well, OK. I mean if you really want to walk,' Flora said, looking slightly hurt.

She had hopped on the bus and stood looking at Leo, her face a picture of concern.

'Thanks for showing me –' she said, then her voice was snatched away by the bus door whooshing shut.

The double-decker juddered away. Leo watched as Flora plopped down in her seat and pushed her nose up against the window, her breath clouding the glass.

She was waving as the bus accelerated away.

Leo knew he could have sneaked on without paying. But he wanted to walk. He wanted some time to think and be on his own.

He supposed he ought to go home.

Leo felt the familiar dread of going home well up, only this time it was worse. Much worse.

Today there would be consequences. Just this once, he wished everything would be as it always was. He'd even settle for Dad out on one of his boozy trips and an empty fridge in an empty house.

It was a long way to walk home but he knew the short cuts. He could cut through alleyways between the houses and down the side of a park. It would take him nearly an hour, maybe, but he didn't care.

As he walked, he passed cosy-looking houses, and through the windows he saw happy mums and dads and normal kids, sitting down for tea.

All his life he had felt like the odd one out. Everybody else had friends round, even just to play video games. Leo couldn't remember ever having a friend home for tea.

He remembered a far-off birthday party. Perhaps he had been six years old or seven. The house had been full of people: friends and mums. He remembered the mums most. How they laughed with each other and clustered in bunches around the table with its small chairs, the kids packed together elbow by elbow munching those tiny squared sandwiches with the crusts cut off.

Where had all the mums gone? he wondered.

He never saw them now.

Somewhere in the distance he thought he heard a siren. Or was it just those birds Mum loved, tilting in the wind? Curlews, he thought she'd called them.

Walking always seemed to help him think. He got into a kind of rhythm which seemed to free his mind.

He was nearing home now, walking along a path between houses with slatted wood fences either side. When he reached the end, he would be in Pier Road at the bottom of the hill. Five minutes and he'd be home.

The quiet of the cut-through gave way to the grim noise of Easthampton's going-home time. The roads were busy. An ambulance passed, its flashing blue light a scary beat.

He began to walk up the hill and realized he was

hungry. He daydreamed of hot dinners like he used to have, before he had to start making his own sandwiches and putting himself to bed.

A fire engine overtook him and he watched its dark hulk speed up the hill. There was no siren. Its lights flashed. It reached the top and disappeared, leaving an aura of flashing blue hanging like a halo in the air.

The ambulance had been silent too. As if the siren was no longer necessary to scare off traffic.

As if it was already where it needed to be. As if it had arrived.

He saw that the glare over the hill was not a flashing light but a growing golden light. Was it gold or was it red? It was red. It was flames; something was on fire.

Then he knew, he knew with absolute certainty that it was his house.

Leo began to run.

His house was on fire.

And there was something precious still inside.

Chapter 13
Save the Box!

Leo ran until he reached the top of the hill and the house came into full, horrific view. The entire front was engulfed in flames and there was a small crowd of people gathered at the end of his drive, milling around, gawping.

High above, a fireman at the end of a giant ladder was sending great arcs of water down on the house from a hose, while below other fire-fighters ran this way and that.

As Leo tried to catch his breath, a great cracking sound came from the front upstairs window. Flames burst through the window as if pushed out by an invisible force. He heard the wood of the window frame fizz and buckle.

Dad's room. It was Dad's room.

Leo's mind was working fast. Where was Dad? He remembered seeing him through his bedroom curtains, lighting his cigarette, remembered how the curtains had closed, shutting like at the end of a play.

'Idiot!' he yelled. And then again, '*Idiot!*'

Anger filled him up. How he hated Dad, he thought. How could he have been so *stupid*! But he felt something else too, something he didn't want to think about. Leo was scared. He was scared that his dad might be injured or even worse. What if? What if . . .?

His mind raced. Thoughts and fears whizzed round his head. He needed to collect himself. He needed to get a grip.

Then he heard a voice in the small crowd. The onlookers had spotted him. They must have heard him shout out.

'The boy! There he is! The doctor's boy, he's alive!'

It was some lady who was shouting, but Leo didn't recognize her. He didn't know her voice and then he saw her break from the group and run towards him.

He had to get away. Quickly Leo pushed through the hedge and into the front garden.

Once through, he crouched down, quite still.

He could hear the calm voice of a fireman, low and steady. He was talking to the lady who had darted towards him, the one who'd spotted him.

'I saw him! I saw the doctor's boy!' she was saying. 'But then he disappeared!'

'At least we know he's safe, madam,' the fireman was saying. 'You've been very helpful.'

Moving quickly, Leo ran round the side of the house, away from the crowd and the fire trucks.

Leo was no longer thinking of his father. He was thinking of the Memory Box.

Everything that was dear to him was in the box. All Mum's memories, all the things she'd wanted him to have. He had to save the box. Whatever the cost. And he had to do it *now*.

In his mind he pictured where the Memory Box was hidden. He could see the white drawers below the chamomile sideboard.

Leo looked up at the house. There above him he could see the balcony outside Mum's room.

At that moment, he felt all fear leaving him. Tonight he would see Mum's room again.

It was impossible to get into the house at the front. He would be seen by the firemen and they would stop him before he even reached the stairs.

So Leo crept round the house to the back. It was there he saw his chance. The kitchen door was ajar, perhaps burst open by firemen or by the heat. Or perhaps Dad had escaped that way.

As he entered the kitchen, there was smoke everywhere, billowing as high as his waist. But Leo knew it was rising. He had little time.

He pulled open drawer after drawer looking for tea-towels to soak in water. Something to cover his face. Finally he found them and pushed them under the cold tap. He held one to his face and made for the stairs.

Then he stopped in his tracks.

Something made him retrace his steps back to the kitchen. He didn't have the key to Mum's room. He would have to break down the door.

He pulled open the cupboards, searching for something – anything – to use. He found Dad's hammer, its yellow plastic handle marking it out in the smoky gloom. As he picked it up, he felt its weight and its rubbery grip.

The smoke was rising. As Leo looked up the stairs, he saw it swirling higher. Yet, strangely, he could see no flames.

Clutching the tea-towel to his face, he ran up the stairs, reaching the three doors on the first landing as quick as he could. Dad's room and his own. Next to them was the bathroom door, which was open. Leo moved swiftly up the stairs again and then he could make out the door to Mum's room on the top landing.

A sudden explosion of noise pinned him down. What on earth was *that*?

When he looked back, he saw there were flames below him, shooting upwards. He was trapped! There was no way down except through the flames.

And yet now, as he stood amid the flames and the smoke and the rising heat, a strange calm took hold of Leo. He felt a kind of peace.

He was alone with Mum now, close to her, near her room and all her things. Whatever happened now he knew was meant to be. He knew it in his heart.

He felt the hammer again in his hand.

Then he saw a movement out of the corner of his eye. Something was moving on the landing down below.

He saw an axe!

A giant axe had burst through Dad's door from the inside. In an instant Leo realized what was happening. The fireman wielding the axe must have been blocked from getting out of the front of the house.

As Leo watched, the axe came crashing through again, and this time he could see the fire raging inside the room.

The masked-up fireman burst through the door, the noise from his breathing apparatus a loud and urgent rasping.

He was carrying Dad!

Leo stood back. They wouldn't see him from here.

Then they were both gone down the stairs.

Beneath him, Leo heard a loud crack and another flame burst upwards from the lower stairs.

There was only one way forward and that was through Mum's door. If he couldn't break through it, the flames or the smoke would claim him. He would die here, locked out of her room.

The door was thick and old, as old as the house. He brought the hammer down – but it just bounced off.

It wasn't working.

For a split second he thought of the people who had died in fires. There must have been so many. Had they all died just like this, convinced they'd be OK until the very end?

The heat was intense now. He didn't have much time.

He decided to aim the blows just next to the handle, where he knew the lock would be.

He slammed the hammer down. Once! Twice! Still it did not move.

He stepped back from the door and charged into it, his right leg straight and high. The door buckled, weakened by the hammer blows, and as he prepared to kick it again it simply opened slowly.

He was inside.

After all this time, he was inside Mum's room.

He took in the scene. Smoke was building in the room. Like a dull cloak rising.

At the end of the room the French windows to the balcony were closed, but something was moving outside. He heard the gasp of hydraulics and firemen's yells.

It was the top of the fire engine's ladder.

Leo looked around, his eyes darting from Mum's

books to her plant pots, to her paintings framed on the walls. The things he had dreamed of for so long.

But his heart was sinking. Everything around him was uncared for. He saw dead plants in dirty pots. In the smoky light he could see rows of dead seedlings in their plastic trays. Nobody had bothered to clean or to water. Nobody had been here for a long time.

The whole room had been left to rot.

How could Dad have given up on Mum like this?

Then he heard the short loud spurts of moving hydraulics and he looked towards the balcony again. Outside the French windows a fireman's head rose above the balcony, like a miner rising from the dark in a pit's lift.

It was Leo's last chance. And yet still he didn't shout out. He didn't run towards the window.

He had a job to do. One job above all else.

He must rescue the box.

Leo moved over to the chamomile sideboard. But it was already hidden beneath the rising smoke. Abandoning the wet tea-towel, he knelt down and burrowed in the smoky heat, pulling out a heavy drawer.

It wasn't there. He felt for it inside, searched for the sharpness of the jewels. But it wasn't there. He couldn't find it.

He tried again. Desperately he pulled open a

second drawer, and then a third, clawing like a blind man, his eyes stinging, crying out in pain.

Then he found it. It was pushed right to the back of the lowest drawer, as far back as it would go. Somehow he could see it through the smoke, he could see Mum's jewels . . .

Leo leant down and wrapped his arms right round it. The jewels pricked into him, but he didn't care.

He saw the writing on the box: *LEO'S MEMORY BOX*.

He saw the picture of him and Mum.

Then reality bit. He had to stand up, he had to get to the French windows and the balcony.

He heaved, trying to bring the box up. But then: disaster!

The box was breaking up. As he pulled it up, he could feel its thin wooden sides bowing open, giving way like cardboard.

But still he hung on, his eyes closed against the smoke.

The box's contents began to spill out. He felt them falling, the box getting lighter and lighter.

One of the sides gaped open and things were still falling out: some of Mum's books and one of her paintings, rolled up and held together by one of those things she used to tie back her hair.

Frantically he grabbed at what he could. He

caught a letter, recognizing it instantly for what it was. One of the birthday letters he had never received.

But it was already black from smoke, its pristine whiteness spoiled by the heat from the fire, some of the writing on the front impossible to read.

Leo pushed it into his trouser pocket.

But still he didn't relinquish the box, his eyes watering from the smoke. He had begun to cough and choke, the smoke inside him.

He had little time; his only chance was the balcony.

Leo made for the French windows, smashing through with all his strength. He was outside, the cold air overpowering.

He saw the fireman, hovering maybe three or four metres away from the balcony on the fire engine's platform.

He was coming towards him fast. Leo noticed the fireman was talking into a radio and then he pulled his mask off and was shouting at him, but Leo couldn't tell what he was saying.

Leo knew he needed to step to the edge of the balcony. He needed to leave Mum's room for the last time or he would die here, die right now.

Then he heard what the fireman was shouting.

'Drop the box! Drop the box!'

Drop the box? Didn't they understand? Didn't they know he'd risked his life to save it? Leo clung on to the box, pulling it in close to him like a mum holds a baby.

He was at the edge of the balcony now, the fireman right in front of him, so near he could touch him.

'I can't fit you on with the box. DROP THE BOX!' the fireman shouted.

Then Leo felt himself being pulled, manhandled over the balcony. Suddenly he was in the fireman's arms. When he looked down, he saw a heavy gloved hand grab hold of the box and try to push it down and away.

'Drop the box, son. Drop it NOW!' the fireman bellowed, his military voice loud and scary.

Is this what happens as you die? Leo wondered. He felt his legs and checked his body. He felt no pain. Is this the way you feel right at the very end?

But he wasn't dying. The fireman's arms were around him and Mum's jewels were glinting in the fire's light.

And then he watched the Memory Box fall into the night.

As the box fell away, he felt something hanging in the air, something cloud-like, all around.

What was it? For a moment he was in among it. Tiny specks of something in the air.

Chapter 14

Lost Property

Leo had been drifting in and out of sleep, and in his dream he could see the sea's ebb and flow, shifting shingle on the beach.

Once he woke sleepily to harsh hospital lights; another time, to a nurse's smile. Later he heard cries of pain from elsewhere. Another's pain, not his own. Then, as he dreamed, he was back in his bedroom, the lights raging and Dad yelling.

He felt the grip of the fireman, felt his overpowering strength pulling Leo away from the balcony. He saw the Memory Box tip into the night, felt his heart breaking as it fell.

Then he dreamed of something else. He dreamed of the letter. The letter from Mum. The one he'd rescued from the fire and pushed into his trouser pocket.

Leo woke suddenly and sat up so fast he felt giddy as the blood rushed to his head.

'MUM'S LETTER!'

Footsteps approached, rapid tip-tapped heels on lino floors. He realized with a start that he must have shouted out loud.

Leo looked up, examining his surroundings, knowing he was in hospital but not knowing where or how he was.

A curtain seemed to be drawn around his bed. Two figures burst through it, crowding into view.

One was a nurse, the other a doctor, his white coat hanging loosely off him as if it was for a bigger man. The nurse began checking his pulse, and speaking to him with a comforting softness.

'Well, well, Leo. You sleep for a whole day and then wake us all up with a healthy shout.'

He noticed the name on her lapel badge. Nurse Celeste Best. She had wrapped a kind of black band so tightly around his arm it pinched. She began to pump it up with a small black balloon, squeezing it to make it work.

'Don't worry, Leo,' she soothed again, 'I'm just taking your blood pressure, that's all. You *have* been in the wars, haven't you?'

Leo grabbed her arm, trying to make himself heard. But he was weaker than he thought.

'Mum's letter!' he said breathlessly. 'Do you know where it is?'

It was as if he was speaking underwater. The words he said didn't seem to make any sense.

He tried again. Trying a different question.

'Where did you put my clothes?'

But the nurse wasn't listening. She was looking over his shoulder. Leo turned to look in the same direction and saw she was reading the screens of the machines by the side of the bed.

'Try to lie still, Leo,' she said. 'There's nothing to worry about, as I'm sure the doctor will tell you. You've been a very lucky young man.'

Leo gazed up at the doctor, who was reading notes taken from a file at the end of his bed. He recognized him. He had seen him before. It was one of Dad's friends. One of his doctor friends. Surely he would help him?

He could even remember his name.

'It's Dr Balfour, isn't it?' Leo said, lifting his head from his pillow.

This time they did seem to hear him. Nurse Best smiled broadly; the doctor seemed impressed.

'You have quite a memory, Leo. The last time I saw you, you were this big . . .'

Dr Balfour spread out his palm about the height of the hospital bed.

'But you've grown up into a very impressive young man. How you got out of that fire we'll never know. You'd practically hidden yourself away at the top of the house, you know. You breathed in a lot of smoke. You may have a sore throat for a while, Leo, feel a bit wheezy. But all in all you've been very lucky; I don't think there'll be any lasting damage.'

The doctor's expression grew more serious.

'Look, Leo, you've had quite a fright, quite a shock. But there are things that need sorting out, things that we need to talk to you about.'

Nurse Best was nodding, tucking in his bedclothes.

'We just need to be sure that you're ready to talk, that's all,' she said, shooting a look at Dr Balfour.

'Now I know you must be very concerned about your father but I'm happy to say he is fine,' the doctor said, smiling. 'He got out of the fire with about as much long-term physical damage as you. In other words, not very much.'

Leo felt a twisting movement in the pit of his stomach. Dad was alive! But strangely he felt no relief, only blankness. He hadn't even thought about Dad.

What kind of son was he that he didn't even care?

His emotions began to churn. All he could do was grab at the nurse's hand. He held it tightly and noticed the way she looked at Dr Balfour, as if she was willing him to say more.

'In fact, your father's not in *this* hospital, Leo,' the doctor continued. 'He hasn't any real physical injuries. He's gone to . . .'

Dr Balfour paused, glancing first at Nurse Best and then at him. Leo felt as if he was being weighed up, as if the doctor was deciding if he was up to hearing bad news.

'He's gone to another kind of hospital,' Dr Balfour continued. 'Somewhere special. Somewhere where we hope he can get better.'

There was a silence while Leo took in the news.

'Another hospital?' he asked. 'What kind of hospital?'

There was movement in the curtains again and another nurse appeared, one Leo hadn't seen before.

'The headmistress is here – you know – Mrs Turner, is it?' she whispered to Nurse Best. 'She's with the other one . . . the one we talked about. Is he OK to talk?'

The new nurse glanced at Leo while he sized her up. She was the kind of grown-up who talked about children as if they were deaf.

Then, before he had time to think about why Mrs Turner would be here at the hospital, she appeared.

She wasn't alone. When she pushed through the curtains, there was another lady. Leo could tell she wasn't a teacher. She had a suit on and a coloured neckerchief. She was tall too and there was something official about her.

'I was just telling Leo,' Dr Balfour said, looking pointedly at Mrs Turner and the other lady, 'that Dad is perfectly fine, physically, but that he has gone to another hospital.'

'How are you, Leo?' Mrs Turner asked. 'We've been worried about you.'

Leo shrugged, not knowing what to say.

'You're a very brave boy, Leo Rake,' she continued.

'You think I'm brave?' he said, his thoughts drifting. He felt so tired. 'Are you sure? Why . . .?'

'You went into that house and tried to save your dad, didn't you?'

Leo nodded vaguely. It was like they were talking about somebody else, not him.

And anyway, it was the box he'd wanted to save.

Leo couldn't take it in. So many thoughts were pressing in, he couldn't focus; his mind began to swim. He began to wonder whether they were preparing him for bad news by telling him something nice first.

It was what adults always did. Like when Dad had told him they could go and see England play at Wembley the day he'd told him Mum had died.

Only they'd never been, had they? To Wembley. It had all been a big fat lie.

Leo lay still, listening to them talking about him. He tuned in and out of what was being said, hearing some of it, trying to ignore the bits he didn't want to hear.

Mrs Turner was talking.

'It was my job, Leo, you see. Once you told me about what was happening at home. Well, once I knew that, I had to ring up Miss Wynnstay here – Liz – I had to ring Liz and tell her.'

Miss Wynnstay spoke with a sing-song voice like this was all fun and normal. But Leo had heard this kind of voice in adults before. He knew her type. The serious type. The ones who made decisions. The bossy ones.

'I'm Liz Wynnstay, Leo. I'm in charge of what we call children's social services here in Easthampton. It's my job to take care of you, to make sure we look at the options.'

Leo's heart sank. The 'options' word again.

He stared up at this Miss Wynnstay, trying to work her out. She wasn't very old, he thought. And she was pretty. Were social workers supposed to be pretty?

Her hair was a kind of yellowy golden colour, and strands of it kept falling across her face and she had to push them back to see. Each time she did so she smiled at him, sort of nervous, like she hadn't done this before, like she was new.

When she spoke again, her voice was a softer sing-song.

'Your dad's going to be away in the hospital for some weeks, you see, Leo, and . . . well, your house needs some repairs, so we have to work out what's best for you. What we thought, Leo, was that one option might be, you could go and stay with your grandmother for a while. Nan, I think you call her.

Then when the big house is ready, you and she could move back into it.'

Leo looked up at the concerned faces. They began to revolve and merge together into one.

'It's a good compromise, Leo, you see – this way, you stay with a member of the family. Then . . . if Dad comes home and everything's all right . . . then maybe we can get back to normal.'

Leo felt like shouting out. But he felt so tired. What did they mean *if* Dad came home?

What did they mean by getting back to normal?

Didn't they realize he couldn't *remember* normal?

Time passed and it was quiet again. Maybe he had fallen asleep. He could not be sure.

When he opened his eyes, everybody seemed to have disappeared. The curtain was still drawn around the bed.

He felt sealed off and safe. He liked the curtains being closed up.

Leo began to think about what the blonde lady, Miss Wynnstay, had said.

He began to think about his dad. And whether he would ever come back.

A special hospital? He knew what that was. He wasn't stupid. Dad had gone to one of those rehab places. He'd heard about those. Wasn't that where famous people went, popstars and the like?

Only Dad wasn't a popstar. He was just a useless drunk who hid his bottles and banged around in the night. Only now he'd really done it. He'd really messed things up. He'd burned down the house and destroyed the Memory Box.

Then he remembered the letter. Remembered he was sure it was here, in the room, close to him.

It must be here, he thought, *somewhere* . . .

But even as he lay thinking he felt sleep creep over him once again, a numbness edging up his body, taking over.

Sometime later Nurse Best appeared through the curtains. He wasn't sure how much later but he knew time had passed. The light seemed different.

She bent down and fluffed up his pillows, producing another from the bottom of the bed so he could sit up properly. She was smiling.

'I've got something for you,' she said, looking over her shoulder, speaking softly so nobody else might overhear them. 'Dr Balfour doesn't know I've checked but you said you wanted your clothes, didn't you?'

Leo nodded, his heart leaping, remembering how he'd stuffed the letter in his trouser pocket.

Nurse Best held up the trousers, which were grimy, almost black. The original light grey impossible to see.

Eagerly Leo grabbed them and plunged his hand

into the pockets. He was sure he'd put the letter in the front left one.

But there was nothing there.

He glanced at Nurse Best.

'Was there anything in the pockets?'

She shook her head. Leo noticed a concerned look come over her face, like she thought she had done something wrong.

'No – was there supposed to be? All the patients' things are sorted out downstairs, you see. They put everything in a plastic bag with your name on it. I checked and they said there was just one thing . . . an old bus ticket. You don't want that, do you?'

Leo was trying the other pockets, turning them inside out so they hung out like white tongues.

Nothing!

He suddenly felt hot all over. He felt faint. Was he going to pass out?

Then he heard raised voices.

'Dr Balfour . . . *Dr Balfour* . . .'

Nurse Best, her head turned away from him, was yelling. Leo heard an urgency in her voice he didn't like. Then he heard whispering. The kind he was used to. The kind he could hear but wished he couldn't.

'. . . very agitated, yes, stressed . . . Yes, I know . . . I'm sorry, Doctor . . .'

Dr Balfour appeared over the nurse's shoulder. He was saying something into her ear.

The last thing Leo remembered was the syringe and the soothing words.

'This will just relax you, Leo . . . make you sleep . . .'

Chapter 15

The Visitor

When Leo woke again, he lay for an age in his narrow hospital bed, putting his jigsaw life together piece by confusing piece.

He could see a clock on the far wall. It was nearing four o'clock. It was light outside so it was afternoon. But which afternoon? He was pretty sure a night had passed since Mrs Turner had come. Her and the other lady.

Leo felt like he had slept forever, but he still felt so tired. His body felt dull and heavy, as if weighed down or made suddenly useless.

A hospital trolley passed close by, its wheels squealing a rackety rhythm.

Jigsaw parts dropped randomly into place. The rolling bottle. Mum's room. He saw the red glow of the lighthouse, moving in silence. He heard the suck of the sea.

Then he remembered the letter. He remembered that it was gone.

Leo felt the sadness then. It came like it had come the day that Mum had died. It was a feeling of emptiness inside, a feeling of sinking, of there being nothing fixed or certain any more.

He felt lonely.

Leo tried to adjust his eyes to the light. He noticed a figure standing by the bed.

'Good afternoon, young man. Are you rejoining us?'

It was Nurse Best. Leo tried to sit up but he felt dizzy.

'Lie back down again,' the nurse was saying, leaning over him, plumping up pillows.

'I must have overslept, I don't remember. How long . . .?'

Nurse Best put her hand on Leo's forehead, trying to calm him. She had produced her thermometer, ready to take his temperature.

'You've had a good night's sleep. We had to give you something, you see, to help you relax . . .'

Leo remembered seeing the needle. It had been like that time at the dentist, when you counted down from ten but never made it.

'. . . but you're right as rain now.'

Leo nodded grimly. She began taking his blood pressure now. He didn't feel as right as rain at all, whatever that meant.

'I have a little boy at home: Charlie,' Nurse Best said as the armband began to pump up and tighten.

'He's just about the same age as you, Leo. Football mad, he is!'

Leo smiled. He liked the sound of this boy.

'Who's his favourite England player?' he said.

The nurse screwed up her face.

'Favourite England player . . . hmmmm . . . Now footie's not my thing. Let me think. He used to like – what's his name? – Ronaldo . . .'

Leo's smile broadened.

'Ronaldo! He's not even English . . . He's Portuguese . . . and he plays in Spain!'

Nurse Best began to laugh.

'Well, I don't know. I just know he likes England and he likes Ronaldo.'

Leo examined the blue and white of her uniform. Everything seemed to be just right about Nurse Best. He bet she was a brilliant mum.

'Anyway, Leo,' she continued, 'I hope Charlie would be as brave as you . . . you know, if something happened to me.'

She was leaning down close to him, speaking quietly, like they were about to hatch a plan.

'Shall I let you into a little secret?' she whispered, turning her head towards the curtains like she was checking for spies.

Leo nodded.

'You had two visitors yesterday, while you were sleeping. Your nan . . .'

Not Nan, Leo thought. Oh no, he didn't want to see her, not yet.

Nurse Best continued: '. . . and a young lady called Flora, says she's your best friend?'

'Flora was here?' Leo said. 'Why didn't you wake me up?'

The nurse chuckled. 'You were out for the count, young man. There was no waking you up.'

Nurse Best's eyes were sparkling. Leo wondered what was coming next.

'She's keen, I'll give her that,' she said, her voice trailing off to a whisper. 'She even came back again today. In fact, she's here right now . . .'

'What, now? Here! Can I see her now? Please . . .' Leo pleaded.

'OK, but you keep it down. The other patients are trying to rest.'

With that, Nurse Best stood back up and was gone, leaving the curtains swishing in her wake. It seemed ages before she returned.

Then there she was! Flora!

'Hello,' she said.

'Hello.'

Flora's duffle-coat was done up like she wasn't staying. Her face looked pink from the fresh air outside. She seemed so alive, too full of energy for this slowed-down place.

'They said I couldn't come at first. They said you'd breathed in loads of smoke.'

Leo listened. It was like she was talking about somebody else.

'But you're OK now? They kept you in, I mean, looked after you . . .?'

Leo had so much he wanted to tell Flora. About Dad going to the other hospital. About having to move in with Nan. About Mum's letter and how it was lost forever. So much he didn't know where to start.

Instead it was Flora who talked.

'I've got some fantastic news – I bet you won't believe it!'

Leo was confused. What did she mean, fantastic news? What *good* news could there be?

'The Prime Minister! He's coming to school. To visit. Like you asked him, Leo. He said *yes*! The email you sent. Remember? It must have got through!'

Leo sat up, his mouth wide open in shock.

'He's coming? So . . . he must have replied to the email –'

Flora was in full flow.

'I don't know about that, but he did ring the school. Manders says he rang Mrs Turner. Isn't it exciting, Leo, isn't it fantastic? I just had to come and tell you.'

At first Leo felt on top of the world. His idea had

worked after all. He had thought of it and now the Prime Minister was coming back to his old school – all because of him.

He didn't look so stupid now, did he? Even Manders would have to give him some credit.

But then he remembered the Memory Box in the fire. He remembered how it had been lost. He felt a sadness returning. It was like a shadow taking away the light.

Leo didn't want to cry, especially not in front of Flora, but once the first hot tear had slipped down his cheek he could tell it was too late. He began to sniff.

'What's the matter, Leo?' Flora said, standing up and searching for a hankie. 'I thought you'd be pleased . . .?'

She offered him a tissue, her eyes wide with concern.

Leo shook his head, trying to find the words.

'It was terrible. In the fire . . .'

Flora leant forward and gripped his arm. She squeezed.

'I suppose you must keep reliving it, going over it again and again,' she said. 'I know all about what happened. Everybody does. The house was gutted, Leo . . . Dad says he drove by it. The windows are all boarded up. There are men there starting the repairs. I bet it will take them ages before –'

She stopped in mid-sentence.

'Where will you live, Leo? Until the house is finished?'

Leo was glum. 'Nan's,' he said, 'I'll have to live with Nan.'

'Well, she should be proud of you, that's all I've got to say,' Flora said.

'Proud?' Leo said, astonished. '*Proud?* What of?'

'Of what you did, silly! In the fire! Everybody knows, like I said. You tried to save your dad, didn't you? You were very brave.'

Leo began to shake his head.

'No,' he hissed, 'you don't understand. Nobody understands. I didn't try to save Dad at all. The firemen saved Dad. I was trying to save . . .

'. . . to save the box.'

Flora sat quite still, beginning to understand.

'The box? You mean you tried to save the Memory Box?'

She stood up and began to pace around.

'So that means . . . you got into your mum's room – the one that was locked up?'

'Yes,' Leo said.

Flora began to look around, her eyes settling on the bedside table and then the cupboard.

'But that's brilliant, Leo. You finally got them,' she said excitedly. 'All those cards and letters from your mum.'

Leo put out his hands to stop her talking.

'That's just it,' he said. 'I found the box but I couldn't save the things in it. The box began to break apart in the heat. I could feel loads of stuff falling out. Then the fireman came and he wouldn't let me save the box. He . . . he made me drop it . . .'

'Drop it. Where?'

'When he took me off the balcony. It just fell . . .'

Flora had a determined look on her face now.

'Talk me through this again, Leo. You were in the room, right?'

'Yes.'

'You found the box but you dropped all the things in it?'

'No – well, yes . . .'

Flora had sat down on the end of the bed.

'Just slow down and tell me what happened.'

'Like I said, I had the box. I found it in the drawer. It was where I remembered it. But it was so hot, you see, and so smoky. I couldn't see much. Not really. But I could feel the heavy things falling out. You know. The books. Diaries and things . . .'

'What happened to them?' Flora said, her voice low and flat.

'I suppose they were burned. I mean, if they fell on the floor they would have, wouldn't they? I had one letter, though, I grabbed it out of the box. I thought I'd put it in my pocket. But it's gone. The nurse says there's no sign of it.'

Flora had turned towards him, her arms folded. She was taking charge.

'This letter,' she said. 'Could it have fallen out of your pocket?'

Leo tried to remember.

'And the Memory Box. It would have dropped into the garden, right? It's probably still there, right?'

Flora had stood up, her face suddenly determined.

'Look, Leo! We've got to go to your house really quickly, you know . . .'

She studied her watch.

'. . . it's after four already. The workmen, the ones repairing the damage. They'll move everything, won't they? We might never find the box if we don't hurry!'

'But how do you know it's there?' Leo protested.

Flora wasn't in any mood to argue.

'Where else can it possibly be?' she said. 'And that letter too – maybe you dropped it there. We won't know if we don't look.'

Flora had opened the tall thin cupboard next to his bed.

'There's a set of clean clothes in here,' she said quietly. 'How are you feeling?'

'Feeling?' Leo echoed, confused. Flora came around the bed and held her hand on his forehead.

'We've got to go, Leo. Now. Don't you see? It's our only chance of saving anything. Maybe nobody else has looked.'

She returned to the cupboard and began handing Leo a set of clothes he didn't recognize. Maybe Nan had put them there – he didn't know.

He began to dress. The jeans were elasticated like for little kids. The shirt was brand new, a big red discount sticker still on its front. He peeled it off and stuck it on the cupboard door.

Flora was getting impatient.

'Come on, Leo! You're just a bit groggy. You'll be fine. There's a whole line of taxis outside. If we grab one, we'll be there in ten minutes.'

She checked her watch.

'It's quarter past four, Leo. It won't stay light forever.'

Chapter 16
In the Garden

The taxi was too big for two. It was a people carrier and they sat facing each other surrounded by empty seats.

'Haven't you got anything bigger?' Leo joked to the driver as they got in.

'First in the queue, son. That's the way it works. You gets what comes up . . .' the taxi driver said, speaking into his mirror, without actually turning around. 'Where to?'

Flora leant forward. 'Hardy's Road. Near the top of the hill. We'll tell you when we get there.'

'Hardy's Road? Tell you what . . . There was a fire there, you know. The other night. At the doctor's house. Nearly killed, he was, so they say . . . Terrible business.'

They said nothing, exchanging only glances.

'Terrible . . .' Flora said.

Leo noticed the way the taxi driver kept glancing

at them. But he seemed to shut up when he started driving. They sat silently.

'What happened when you got home?' Leo said eventually. 'After we went to the cemetery. What did your dad say?'

They were turning off the main road into the street that led to Leo's house. The tick-tocking of the indicator a hypnotizing pulse.

'Me and Dad had a long chat,' Flora said. 'About you.'

'About me?'

'Well, yes. You and your dad. About what it must have been like . . . Dad says your dad sounds a lot like Mum.'

Flora smiled and, reaching out, held his arm just for a second.

'He says you need looking after. That . . . that it must have been very tough. Having to cover up and everything. But he said that maybe, now, maybe everybody knows . . . maybe it's a relief too?'

Leo looked down at the taxi's floor, not knowing what to say. Somebody had thrown an empty crisp packet down and tried to kick it under the driver's seat.

'What about at school? What did they say about it there?'

They were on Hardy's Road now. Flora was leaning forward, her head between the two front seats, checking where they were through the windscreen.

She turned back to face him. 'Everybody's talking about it. People were saying horrible things. Like you'd had all your skin burned off.'

Leo was horrified. 'But I haven't . . .'

He held out his arms as if to prove it.

'That wasn't all they said either. They said your dad was trapped in the house and that you saved him –'

'Well, that's just rubbish,' Leo said. 'Like I said, I . . .'

The car was beginning to slow. It was making its way up the hill.

'Dad says people always talk. He says they've nothing better to do,' Flora soothed. 'If they don't know, they make it all up.'

Leo wanted to ask more questions. But Flora was speaking to the taxi driver.

'Just drop us here.'

Leo was puzzled. This wasn't the house. They hadn't even got over the brow of the hill yet.

'But – this isn't . . . It's not –' he protested.

Flora shushed him, a finger on her lips, her eyes widening.

'Here. Here will be fine,' she said, all matter of fact, as if she jumped in and out of cabs all the time.

The driver had slowed to a stop.

'OK, princess,' he said. 'Here you are . . .'

Leo had to slide the door to get out. He stood on the path, waiting while Flora paid the driver. He had to admit she did a good impression of a grown-up.

'Why did you hush me up?' Leo asked. 'I was only asking why we were stopping here when my house is *there*.'

'Well, we could hardly stop in front of yours,' Flora replied, glancing over his shoulder as a car lumbered by, its lights lit for the approaching evening. 'It's a deserted house, remember.'

'But why do we have to pretend?'

'Didn't you hear what he said? He knew all about the house. Don't you think he'd have thought it a bit odd if we'd got out there? We don't want to be disturbed, do we?'

They were walking now, up to the brow of the hill. Leo began to see Flora's point.

'He *was* looking at us a bit strange . . .'

The house loomed out of the gathering dark, a great hulk, unlit and empty.

It didn't look like his house at all. It looked dead, somehow, as if it had never been a home to anyone, let alone him.

Leo pushed open the gate and when they had both gone through he looked up at the front of the house.

'Oh lordy . . .' he said. 'What a total mess . . .'

146

The windows of the house had all been boarded up, just like Flora's dad had said.

All around them were workmen's things, a bench with another hoarding on it, ready to be cut to the right size.

There were teacups everywhere. Discarded hard hats ready for work tomorrow.

'They didn't waste any time, did they?' Leo said. 'They look like they've been here forever.'

A yellow skip stood in the drive with a great chunk of masonry sticking out. He recognized it. It was the window frame from Dad's room.

Flora was shaking her head.

'There's no way we can get inside. Even if we wanted to . . . Look!'

They were at the front of the house. Two great planks of wood had been put in a 'X' shape across the front door. On one of them a sign had been nailed:

Danger! Keep Out!

Leo stared at what had been his front door. The brass plaque on the wall was black with sooty dust but when he rubbed it over with his hand it came up shiny.

'Well done, *Doctor* Rake,' he said under his breath.

'What?' Flora said absent-mindedly. She was standing back, looking up at the house.

Leo knelt down and found the key in its hiding-place.

'Look what I found!' he said in a self-mocking voice. 'A key to a door that's all blocked up. There's hardly any actual house behind it but I've . . . I've got the key!'

Leo waved it in the air like it was a prize.

Flora put her hand on his shoulder and changed the subject.

'It looks like a tank rolled through here,' she said. 'Look at these churned-up tracks.'

Leo looked at the front garden, trying to remember what it had looked like before.

'The fire engine must have come into the drive and then backed up in front of the house,' he said, piecing things together. 'I bet that was the only way they could get the ladder up to me.'

He pointed up towards Mum's room. They began to walk round the house into the main part of the garden.

'I was at the side of the house, see. That's Mum's balcony up there. Behind the little wall.'

They both looked up. The wall below the balcony was scarred and blackened by the fire.

'So when you dropped the box, you must have dropped it right . . .' Flora walked purposefully to the bit of grass right under the balcony. '. . . here.'

They both looked. There was nothing there.

'Why's the grass so long anyway?' Flora said. 'Doesn't it ever get cut?'

Leo could remember when the grass was cut short and neat. When there were bare, bald patches of grass at either end of the garden where he and Dad had their pyjama footie goals.

But that was a long time ago.

Now there was just overgrown grass. And rose bushes that never grew roses.

A feeling of hopelessness crept over him, a sinking of the soul.

'It's all a waste of time, this!' he said suddenly, his hands on his hips. 'There's nothing left here. It's all been burned to nothing or smashed up by the men or –'

'Oh, *do* shut up, Leo!' Flora snapped. 'We've got to at least *try*, haven't we? I mean, the box can't have vanished into thin air . . .'

Flora knelt down and began to move her hands through the grass.

'Come on, you! I can't do this all on my own,' she said, smiling to show she was still his friend.

For a time the two of them worked, side by side, flattening the grass as they went to show which bits had been searched.

But if there ever had been anything, it wasn't there any more.

After a while Flora stood up, dusting grass off her duffle-coat.

'What time is it?' Leo said. 'Won't it be getting dark soon?'

'It's nearly half past five,' she said.

There was still light in the garden, but it wouldn't last for long. They stood together and looked out towards the sea. A half-moon hung high.

Leo stood up, holding his arms out at his side, his fingers spread out like a footballer appealing to a referee.

He felt tired. All he wanted to do was just go home. Only this *was* his home. Or used to be.

But Flora was made of sterner stuff.

'Don't you think we should go down and inspect the rose bushes?' she said. 'Maybe something could have blown down there and got caught on the thorns.'

'Like what?' Leo asked, unconvinced.

Flora was staring down the garden, her hand raised to her forehead in a flat salute.

'Why not? It must have gone somewhere.'

Leo laughed. Only it wasn't a funny-ha-ha laugh, it was a flat laugh. The kind grown-ups made when things weren't funny.

'What about the letter? It could have blown anywhere.'

'What – you think the letter had wings?' Leo said, irritated now. 'The roses are miles away . . .'

But Flora wasn't having any of it. She was walking purposefully now, making Leo keep up.

'There's no need to be rude, Leo. I don't see any point in giving up. Do you?'

Leo hung his head. He wasn't sure why he was arguing.

'Just a minute!' Flora said all of a sudden. 'What's this?'

Leo ran to her side. There was some kind of charred paper in the grass, a fragment from the fire.

But when she picked it up, he could see it was useless. He couldn't even tell what it was.

'Told you . . .' he said in a moaning voice. 'This is all a waste of time.'

Flora stopped and stood still, her arms folded like one of the teachers in the playground about to deliver a lecture.

'Do you know what your trouble is, Leo Rake?' she said, sticking out her bottom lip.

He shook his head.

'You give up too easily, that's what.'

Leo began to laugh. He knew she was right.

'OK, OK . . . Sorry,' he smiled.

'What's on the other side of the roses anyway?' Flora asked, trying to be as cheery as possible.

They were nearing the roses now. They could see the thorny tubers, unkempt and intertwining.

'South Green,' Leo said.

'South Green? You mean the common?' Flora repeated.

Leo remembered Flora was still quite new to Easthampton.

'Yes. It's the common that goes down to the seafront. There's the guns there, you know, the old black ones. Then there's just the beach huts.'

Leo brightened, a warm memory cheering him.

'We used to go down there all the time. We had a hut, you see . . .'

Flora brightened too.

'A beach hut! You never said . . . What colour is it painted? Does it have a name?'

Leo pictured Mum's hut. It made him feel sad again.

'Lion's Den,' he said quietly.

Flora seemed to sense his change of mood. Her eyes were wider, registering concern.

'Lion? I don't understand,' she said, pushing her hair away from her face.

'It's what they called me when I was little. *Lion*, you see, as in *Leo*.'

Flora smiled.

'Anyway. The hut's not up to much these days. It's like everything around here,' he said quietly. 'It's gone to rack and ruin. I remember it used to be a bright white colour with blue bits round the edges. But it's all tatty now. Nobody's bothered to look after it.'

They were standing on tiptoe, looking over the roses and, behind them, the hedge. Beyond it South Green rolled this way and that, like an unfinished golf-course.

Here and there were houses a bit like Leo's. Plonked down in the middle of the Green and surrounded by gardens.

Then beyond the houses was a long white metal fence, like you only get at seaside places, marking out the line where the land falls away towards the beach.

It had begun to spit with rain. A cold breeze furrowed the untidy grass and set the empty roses chattering.

Leo gazed out to sea. A fishing boat put-putted towards the harbour. When he glanced back at Flora, he saw she had turned and was looking at the house.

He looked back towards the sea. The seagulls rocked and rode above the Green, sweeping down between the houses.

Then, all of a sudden, Flora grabbed his arm.

'Look! Up there!' she said. 'In the tree. Something white!'

Leo felt his spirits soar. Flora was pointing towards the oak tree near the house.

'Just there. In the branches. Can't you see?'

She was right! He could see them now. First he saw one, then another. Scraps of paper hanging in the branches.

They were bigger than the scrap they'd found in the grass. And there were loads of them. How could they have missed them before?

'Can you lift me up?' Flora yelled, reaching the tree first.

Leo tried to lift her. But it was no use. The branches were just too high.

'I've got a better idea!' he yelled, jumping up and catching a low branch. 'Grab one of these and shake.'

Leo began to jump up and down while Flora ran back and looked up at the paper.

'Keep shaking!' she said, excitedly. 'Here comes one . . . now!'

Leo and Flora ran so fast towards the falling paper thcy nearly collided.

It fell lightly, fluttering down. In the end Flora just picked it out of the air.

'Let me see,' Leo yelled, watching Flora turn it round and round in her hand.

But the light had gone from Flora's face. He could see she was disappointed.

'It's just a bit of paper burned at the edges . . .' she said slowly.

As she spoke, a second fluttered down and then another. Soon the air was full of paper.

Leo grabbed one, then another, looking for pen marks, writing, anything.

One looked like a page from a book.

Flora had found another and handed it to him. He recognized it now. It was from one of Mum's books, a poem she had tried to read him but he'd never understood.

'What's it say?' Flora asked, turning one of the burnt scraps around, trying to make sense.

'East Co – ker,' she read. 'What's that mean? East Coker?'

'Something from one of her poetry books,' he said, taking the piece of paper.

He noticed there was an 'I' below the words – the Roman numeral, like it was a verse.

Flora tried to be breezy again.

'We can find it on the Internet. Check it out. I bet you'll remember then,' she said.

Leo folded it up and put it safely away, patting his pocket to make sure it was there.

'Sorry, Leo,' Flora said, 'getting your hopes up and everything.'

Leo looked up at the other trees. The beech trees on the other side. The elm at the front. There were scraps of paper in all of them like some ticker-tape parade had passed.

They began to trudge back down the garden.

'Do you want to come back to ours?' Flora asked. 'I'm sure Dad will be OK. You know. He'll understand.'

Leo just shrugged.

'Guess so . . .' he mumbled. 'Not that it'll make much difference. Nan will track us down. I'm supposed to be in hospital, remember!'

The rain was getting worse. Instead of spitting it was beginning to pour down.

They started to run. Soon they were round the corner in front of the house, the sodden, churned-up grass slowing them down.

Leo never knew quite why he tripped or what he tripped on. Maybe it was Flora's heel. Maybe it was something sticking up from the mud.

What he would always remember was the feeling he was going to hurt himself. That he was out of control – still running, but with his legs taken from under him. He tried desperately to right himself, unable to see properly because of the rain.

He hit the skip at full speed, his hands held out to stop himself. He clattered into its side, a hollow clang signalling his arrival.

'Oh, Leo . . . are you OK?'

Flora was kneeling down, her hands placed on either shoulder.

Leo felt an anger swelling.

'What else can go wrong?' he yelled. The rain echoed against the skip.

He struggled up, pushing Flora away, just wanting to get away. To be anywhere! Anywhere but here.

He stood up, his body stiff and sore.

Only then did he glance inside the skip. Only then did he see it.

The Memory Box!

It was squashed down to the side of the window frame. It looked shrunken somehow, sad and abandoned. But it *was* the box. He was absolutely sure!

He turned to yell at Flora to get her to look. But when he tried to shout, no sound came out.

She was making her way towards the little path and the gate.

His voice returned in a rush.

'WAIT!' he yelled. 'I'VE FOUND IT. IT'S HERE!'

He looked back into the skip. The dirty, blackened jewels on the box's top glinted at him. Mum's jewels!

'Let me look!'

Flora was running up behind him, her voice raised above the rain.

Leo knew he had to get into the skip. There was one low side, where the workmen threw things in.

When he looked inside he saw rainwater was gathering. It was like a lake in there.

Just as he was climbing in, Flora caught up with him. She held on to him, peering in, eager to see.

'Be careful,' she said. 'There's glass in there.'

Leo picked his way towards the box. The window frame from Dad's room had been slung in the middle, its white paint blackened by the flames. Flora was right. Shards of glass still clung to the frame, jagged and sharp.

The box was on its side. When he picked it up, he felt the sides give, like they had in the fire.

It didn't take him long to retrace the few steps back. He passed the box over to Flora, who took it carefully.

'Open it up,' he said. 'I need to check for the other things.'

'Other things?' Flora said. There was rain dripping from her hood and even from her nose.

'Yes. The letters, remember, the birthday cards. This rain will spoil everything. This could be our last chance.'

Flora lifted up the lid. As she did so, Leo could see the words written on the top, the ones Mum had written years ago.

LEO'S MEMORY BOX

The photo of the two of them looked like it had aged a thousand years. But he could still make Mum out, still see himself. They looked like a boy and his mum from olden times.

Flora was peering into the box. She was shaking her head.

'There's nothing here . . .' she said.

Leo turned to search the skip.

'Except for this?'

When Leo glanced back over his shoulder, his heart dropped.

It wasn't a letter. It wasn't even an envelope.

'What is it?' he said, his hands on his hips.

Flora twirled whatever it was around her index finger.

'I think it's a scrunchie,' she said.

'A scrunchie! What's a scrunchie?'

'Girls put them in their hair. You know. At the back. To tie it up. It must have got in there by mistake.'

Leo felt the water coming over his shoes, soaking his socks. He didn't think he had ever been as wet as this.

But suddenly he didn't care. Suddenly he remembered where he'd seen the scrunchie before.

'What . . . what colour is it?' he said, peering through the rain at whatever was in Flora's hand.

Flora was shaking it. 'Well, it's all black now . . . but I think it – I think it was pink . . . Look!'

Leo could see clearly now. Flora was holding it up. It *was* pink.

Leo picked up the window frame and began to push it as hard as he could, levering it up.

'What are you doing?' Flora yelled. 'Have you gone mad?'

But Leo wouldn't stop. Soon he had stood the frame up on its side and then, when he pushed it one last time, it smashed down on the side of the skip and vaulted out into the mud.

'Don't you see?' he said, breathless. 'That band,

that scrunchie, or whatever you call it. It was inside the box. She used them to hold together her paintings after she rolled them up, for safe-keeping, see . . .'

Flora was looking past him, her eyes searching the skip.

'So if the scrunchie survived the fire,' she said, 'then maybe the picture did too . . .?'

'The scrunchie *was* in the box, right?' Leo asked.

Flora nodded.

'So the picture must have been as well. It must be here. In the skip.'

Flora clambered in. Soon the two of them were moving methodically between what was left of the debris.

It was easier now. Leo guessed the workmen's first job had been to dump in the window frame from Dad's room. There didn't seem to be that much else in there yet.

It was just a matter of time . . .

'There!' Flora shouted triumphantly, bending down to pick something up.

Leo swivelled.

He saw, immediately, that it *was* one of Mum's paintings. Flora was holding it aloft like a prize. It was still rolled up, tight, but it had bent in the middle. It glistened in the rain and he could see it was soaked and dripping.

'Let's get out!' Leo shouted, making to pick his way back.

Flora was pulling at him.

'The letter!' she said through the rain. 'Don't you want to search for that too?'

But Leo was certain.

'There's no way,' he said. 'Look. You can see to the bottom of the skip. All of it. It's obvious there's nothing else. Anyway, think about it. The picture only survived because somehow it stuck in the box. I *had* the letter. It was in my pocket, remember.'

Leo helped Flora step over the angled edge of the skip. Then he climbed out after her.

She handed him the picture, her eyes glowing.

'Let's have a look!' she said. 'What's the painting of?'

Leo examined it. He realized he had no idea. Mum was always painting things.

'I . . . I don't know,' he said, trying to unfurl it. 'But, look, it's sticking together. It's too wet to open up . . .'

Handing the picture to Flora, a new determination swept over Leo.

'Come on!' he shouted. 'Let's go! Let's get out the rain . . .'

Flora pursed her lips. Leo had begun to walk away. Only he wasn't walking towards the gate and the road beyond. He was walking in the opposite direction.

'Where are you going?' she shouted after him. 'My house is that way.'

'But we're not going to your house. There's somewhere else we can go.'

Flora began to run after him, clutching the rolled-up picture.

'Where? Where are you going?' she shouted.

'The hut, of course!' he yelled back. 'Come on!'

Chapter 17

Lion's Den

They were on the prom, a narrow path along the seafront. They walked between the sea and the first of the huts, side by side.

Leo narrowed his eyes and looked seawards. The salt wind was ripping in and the rain lashed down.

The sea seemed angry. Wave after wave broke out of the darkening sky, white crests standing high then hurtling towards the shore.

A light flashed. A piercing white and then, as he looked up, a red light humming in its wake. The lighthouse!

Flora held on to his arm, gripping tightly.

'Which one is it?' she shouted above the roar, her head nodding towards the row of huts.

You could see the bright colours even in the storm. One was painted red with white stripes. Another a navy blue with purple doors and windows. The colours were wild and free.

It had always been like this in Easthampton, for

as long as Leo could remember. The huts had names too.

'Here it is. It's this one!' he shouted.

They had stopped outside a sorry-looking hut, browny coloured, its paint peeling and uncared for.

Leo guided Flora up the two steps that led to the small deck, offering some protection from the driving rain.

'Doesn't anybody ever come here?' Flora said, pushing back her hood. 'It looks so – well – rickety and old.'

Leo was squatting down, his hand feeling down at the side of the deck.

'What are you doing?' Flora asked.

'Looking for the key. We used to keep it under a brick . . . just . . . just here.'

It was a small key attached to a key-ring and a clunky piece of wood. He handed it up to Flora who began to jiggle it in the lock.

She didn't seem to be able to open it.

'Let me have a go,' Leo said, taking over. 'I remember Mum saying there was a knack to it.'

The lock clicked and he pushed the door. When it opened, it scraped the floor like it didn't quite fit the frame any more. Like it hadn't been opened for ages.

It felt musty inside, like an old shed. But at least it was dry.

Leo's hand searched for the light. He remembered there had been a piece of string hanging down. He pulled it.

The light came on.

Memories came rushing back. Leo remembered bright white wooden walls. The doors thrown open on sunny days.

'This place needs a lick of paint,' Flora was saying. 'And just look at the dust! It's like Miss Havisham's room with no Miss Havisham.'

'Miss Havisham?' Leo said, the name only vaguely familiar.

'Oh, *you* know. In *Great Expectations*. We did it with Manders . . . She stayed in her wedding dress forever in her dusty room. You're good at English. I thought you'd remember.'

Leo glowered. He loved reading books, just like Mum had done. But lately Manders had put him right off it.

He thought of Mum and how she loved to read. How she'd said it made her glow inside.

'We used to come here. Mum and me . . .'

'Can you remember? Coming here, I mean?' Flora said.

He screwed up his face.

'Not really . . . She got ill, you see, ages ago. Way before she died. She couldn't come here any more. I'd almost forgotten about it.'

Leo glanced around. He could tell the walls used to be white. But now they were the same colour as outside. A dreary off-white brown. There didn't seem to be anything in the hut at all. Just a beaten-up chest of drawers in front of the back wall.

Flora had gone over and began to open one of the drawers.

'Hey, look, there's something in here,' she said. 'It's an old photograph. It's . . . hey, Leo . . . is this your mum and dad?'

She came over and handed it to him, her eyes studying his.

'Look at them together,' Flora said. 'That *is* your mum and dad, isn't it? Oh, Leo. They look so happy.'

Leo looked at the picture. It was Mum and Dad all right. But he didn't recognize anything else about it.

'Why've they got dressing-gowns on?' he wondered out loud.

The picture showed two people sitting together on a plush red sofa covered with cushions. In front was a low marble table with a tray of cakes in the middle, like in a posh café, a large plate at the bottom and then another above and small one still above that.

'Look how they're cuddling and smiling for the camera,' Flora whispered. 'They look – well . . . they look so in love.'

This was a mum and dad that Leo didn't know.

He could only remember arguments. He remembered being the one in the middle trying to stop the shouting.

'Yes,' he said, 'I suppose they were once. Weren't they? Happy, I mean?'

'Of course,' Flora said, smiling. 'Mums and dads have to be in love, don't they? Or there wouldn't be children, would there? There wouldn't be you! They loved each other all right. Just look at them.'

The rain was drumming on the roof.

'Bet I know why they're laughing!' he said suddenly. 'I've worked it out.'

He held out the photo to Flora.

'I remember Dad used to do this, before – you know . . . He took the photo himself, see, on one of those delay things. He must have put it down, on a cupboard or something, and run back. Look – he's just jumped back on the sofa!'

Flora giggled.

'They're having such fun,' she said. 'He looks so handsome, your dad. And your mum. She was so . . . pretty. Look at her. She's really beautiful.'

Leo wanted to put the photo somewhere safe. He opened the top drawer again and put it in, closing it up.

He noticed the painting. Flora must have put it on top of the chest. Gingerly, he picked it up, but it had begun to unfurl on its own.

'Be careful!' Flora whispered. 'Roll it out on the side, I'll hold down this end.'

Flora put her hands on two of the corners and Leo slowly unfurled it, keeping it flat on the side.

'Wow!' Flora exclaimed. 'She could paint, couldn't she . . .'

It was one of Mum's flower paintings. Leo recognized the view instantly. It was a picture of the garden.

'It's what she could see from the balcony . . .' Leo said slowly. 'Look – you can even see the huts in the distance and the sea.'

A shiver went down Leo's spine.

'Look at the rose garden!' Flora said, excitedly. 'Look at the colours. Is that what it was really like, Leo?'

But Leo wasn't answering. Instead he was peering at the picture. Staring at something he'd seen behind the rose garden. A small figure playing with a ball by the hedge.

'Look!' he whispered. 'I think that's me . . . there in the grassy bit. I remember –'

He looked up.

'– I remember I used to play down there and wave up at Mum . . . Look! It *is* me.'

In Leo's head he heard the breeze blowing through the rose bushes. He heard Mum's voice . . .

'*Le – o!*'

She was shouting for him to come in for tea.

Then there was a knocking sound.

Knock! Knock!

There it was again.

Flora had heard it too. There was someone at the hut door.

There was a voice too.

'Are you in there, Leo Rake? That taxi driver said he dropped you around here. I knew you'd –'

The door burst open. It was Nan.

'Right, young lady,' she bustled, on seeing Flora. 'You can get on straight home. I've had your dad on. He's worried sick – if it hadn't been for the taxi driver, I don't know *where* we'd have looked for you.'

Flora had quickly rolled the picture up and put it in the drawer. When she closed it, she leant on it for good measure.

'Well, don't just stand there, missy – off you go – come on!'

Flora mouthed a goodbye to Leo.

'Off home!' Nan snapped. 'Now!'

She turned her attention to Leo. 'As for you, my lad – what on earth did you think you were doing, just running out of hospital like that? You're coming home with me straight away . . . You'll catch your death.'

Nan held the door open for them so they both had to bow their heads to get under her arm. As they left, Leo leant over and tugged the light pull.

They had walked on a few yards when Leo remembered the key. It was still in his pocket.

'I need to go back. The key,' he said. 'I haven't put it back.'

But Nan's glare was enough to convince him there was no going back tonight.

Leo looked back at the hut. He noticed a warm glow coming from under the door.

He was sure he'd switched the hut light off. He was certain of it.

That light . . . hadn't he seen that light somewhere before?

Chapter 18

Nan's Story

Nan was trying her best to be cheery – he had to give her that. But it didn't really suit her.

She even smiled at him, now and again, on their way to her house. Making allowances.

Nan's front door opened straight into the front room, a small sitting-room that smelt of stew.

Did they sell old-lady stuff at special old-lady shops, Leo wondered? Did it come in granny kits? Lace doilies for the backs of chairs. Pink rugs that fitted around the toilet in the loo.

And when did they give it out anyway? Nan wasn't as old as other people's grandmas, he knew that. She was still fit as a fiddle. Maybe they gave the granny kits out with the bus-pass she got and kept in her purse with the photo of Dad.

'Come through, Leo,' Nan said, her voice lowered to fit the small rooms. 'I'll put the kettle on.'

Leo liked Nan's kitchen. Everything was always

the same. Even though it was only evening, the table was set for breakfast. Set for one.

A cereal bowl stood on a mat. A spoon next to it, polished and ready. A bare toast rack on a tiny tray next to a marmalade jar, waiting for morning.

Nan busied herself, opening and closing cupboards.

'We shall need this in the morning, shan't we?' she said, more to herself than Leo, a second cereal bowl in her hand.

She paused.

'Or do you want just toast,' she said, 'because if you want just toast I shall have to get another plate out . . . And a knife.'

Nan turned away towards the cupboard.

'Or maybe you want both. Cereal *and* toast. I don't know what you have for breakfast these days, do I . . .?'

She stood looking at Leo, her lips pursed.

'I mean, you don't stay here often, do you?'

Leo shook his head.

'Cereal or toast? Come on. What will it be?' Nan said.

It occurred to Leo that Nan's world was different from his. It existed in a parallel universe organized one day ahead of events.

'Can't I decide in the morning?' he said.

Nan looked at Leo like he was a stranger. Then she forced a quick smile. He could tell she was trying her best to be kind.

'What's the matter with me?' she said suddenly, as

if waking up from a daydream. 'You need to get out of those wet clothes. What have you been doing – rolling around on the ground?'

Nan appeared to be thinking. Something told Leo this was bad news.

'*I* know. Let's pop up to Tommy's room.'

'*Tommy's* room?' Leo echoed. 'You mean Dad has a room . . . here?'

'I should hope he did, young man. This is where he grew up – remember!'

The stairs at Nan's were narrow, so as they walked up them she had to go first, leading the way. Leo wondered why it was he hadn't ever been here much. He knew he'd been upstairs, but he couldn't remember the last time.

At the front of the house was Nan's room. They stood on the small landing with the bathroom door ajar. Next to it, facing towards the back of the house, was another door.

'This was Tommy's room . . . Your dad's room. When he was, well, when he was your age,' Nan said, pushing down the handle.

The room had the smell of an unused room, its life on hold.

Leo looked around.

The bed was made tightly, packaged like a parcel. The walls were white, anonymous, like all the personality had been painted away.

Nan opened the clothes cupboard, a large dark-wood dresser that seemed too big for the room.

'Now then. Let's see what we've got in here . . . I don't like to throw things away, you know. There's a lot of your dad's things, you see. Things he wore when he was your age. I don't see why they wouldn't fit.'

Leo frowned. He wished he could go back to the house and grab something out of the scruffy cupboard where he'd hidden the bottles. Anything would do. At least they were *his* things.

Nan was sliding coat-hangers along a rack.

'Here we are. What about this?' she said. 'You like football, don't you?'

This was a turn-up! Nan was holding out an England football shirt, as white and as ironed as the day it had been bought.

At least he *thought* it was an England shirt. It was just about the right colours and it had the three lions of England on the front, the famous badge.

But everything else about the shirt was weird. For starters, the kit name. *Admiral*. Who was Admiral when they were at home?

'Was this Dad's?' Leo said, turning it round. On the back was a giant number eleven.

'Where's the name?'

Nan was on the landing, then in the tiny bathroom. She was starting to run a bath.

But Leo could still hear her. That was the good thing about small houses.

'What name?' she shouted.

Leo looked at the shirt again. It was V-necked and white, mainly. At the top on the front there was a deep blue stripe and then the red one below it, narrower. Then underneath that was a smaller stripe going right across. A blue one.

He turned it around again.

'The name of the player, of course!' he yelled.

'There's no need to shout now,' Nan said. She had walked back into the room, leaving the sound of water gushing into the bath behind her.

'Did you not pay for the name to be put on the back? Is that it?' Leo said. 'I bet that's it.'

Nan took the shirt. She held it up, examining it.

'I may be wrong, young man, but I'm not sure we did that kind of thing back then. The names and such.'

Leo was dubious. After all, if they didn't have names on the backs of shirts, how would the commentators know who was who?

'Come on!' Nan said briskly. 'Let's get you in the bath.'

A few minutes later Leo lay in the warm water, letting the bubbles tickle him. The sound of plates and knives and forks downstairs was somehow comforting.

He heard Nan coming back upstairs. She peeped round the bathroom door, which was made of white-painted slatted planks and had an old-fashioned handle on it – like a door you get outside, not inside.

'Can I come in?'

She was waving something white, like she was surrendering.

'Are these any use?' she said.

It was the shorts for the England kit. They had the number eleven on in red and the Admiral thing on too. They looked quite smart, he thought, with their red and white stripes down either side.

'Tomorrow we'll have to go to the shops. Get you some things.'

Leo laid back and splashed some water over his face. He didn't mind Nan being in the bathroom. Not really.

'Oh – I found something else,' she said suddenly, disappearing.

When she came back, she was holding something folded up. He could tell it had been a poster because on one of the corners there was some old Blu-Tack.

'Tommy had this on his wall. I had the room painted, you know, over the years. But I kept this – well, I suppose I just couldn't throw it away . . .'

Leo unfolded it. For a second he thought it was a picture of a girl. But it wasn't. It was just that the player had long hair. He had the same England kit

on, the one with the Admiral badge. And he was
wearing the number eleven.

'Paul Mariner,' Leo read the words out loud,
'Ipswich and England.'

He looked at Nan, chuckling.

'*Ipswich?!*'

Nan was laughing too now. Leo noticed how nice
she looked when she laughed.

'He was his favourite, Paul Mariner was . . .'

'But Ipswich and England, Nan? Didn't this
Mariner play for one of the big clubs? I mean,
Ipswich is near here. How can an England player
live near here?'

'Well, I don't know about that but I do know he
played for Ipswich. I remember Tom took your dad
once. To . . .' She frowned.

'Portman Road,' Leo said. 'I know all the grounds.
I've got them on my footie cards. You can test
me . . .'

Nan held out a big towel. Leo stood up and let her
wrap him up in it. He couldn't remember being
cuddled by Nan before. But he liked it. It made him
feel safe.

'Let's get you downstairs and get a cup of tea
inside you,' she said. 'I've got some food on too.'

Leo knew what was coming next.

'Stew,' she said. 'I made it special.'

* * *

The front room was warmer now. Homely.

Leo eyed Nan's old computer, which was on a small desk near the bottom of the staircase.

'Oh, Nan . . . Can I use the computer? I need to –'

Nan interrupted.

'Later maybe,' she chided. 'We've got lots of time for that. Remember, you're going to be living here for a bit.'

Nan had taken out the middle table from a small nest of light-wood tables next to the sofa. She pushed it along the thick carpet, positioning it right in front of Leo.

'There. We can have a chat while you eat,' she said, disappearing back to the kitchen.

'Am I going to live here for long?'

'I suppose that depends . . . on how long it takes to repair the house. I mean, we can both move in there for a bit when it's ready. We'll have more space.'

Nan put a large plate of steaming stew in front of him.

'Anyway, when your dad comes back –'

Leo had begun to eat, only suddenly he didn't feel very hungry.

'I know where Dad's gone, you know,' he said. 'He's gone –'

Nan was blinking. Leo wondered if she had something in her eyes.

'The doctor told me, the nice one in the hospital. Dr Balfour.'

Leo realized Nan wasn't blinking at all. She was trying not to cry.

'I'm worried about Tommy,' she said under her breath. 'I've been worried about my Tommy for a long, long time . . .'

Leo made to interrupt, but stopped himself. Nan was looking into space as if she was talking to someone else. But he could see she wanted to talk, wanted to get things off her chest.

'They've taken Tommy away to try to make him better. They've taken him to a place called Promise. It's out in the country a long way away.

'They rang me up to tell me. It's what they call a re-hab-il-it-ation centre . . .'

Nan pronounced each bit of the word as if it didn't belong in her mouth, as if it wasn't possible that she could say it.

'It's because my Tommy's what they call an alcoholic.'

A couple walked past in the road. Their arms interlinked. Leo could make them out through Nan's net curtains.

Nan's moist eyes fixed on his.

'Do you know what an alcoholic is?' she asked, tears marking her face.

Leo thought of the nights of hiding bottles. He

thought of the shouting and the stink, the never knowing which dad he'd see when he got home from school.

He nodded.

Nan seemed to stare at him a moment, then looked away.

'He has to stay there for weeks, does Tommy . . . in the re-hab-il-it-ation place. They say he won't be a doctor ever again unless he stops the drink. They won't let us visit either, not yet – not till they decide it's all right . . .'

Nan stopped for a minute and closed her eyes, like she was reaching into the past to find her memories.

'They didn't have a rehab for my Tom,' she whispered.

Now Leo really was lost. What *was* she talking about?

'*Tom?*' Leo asked. 'Who's Tom?' But he was suddenly sure he'd heard the name not long before.

Nan opened her eyes and looked straight at him.

'Tom was your grandad,' she said, her eyes beginning to well up. Leo realized that he had never seen Nan cry.

Then again he'd never really talked to Nan. Not properly. Until now.

'You never talk about Grandad,' he said. 'He died. Didn't he? In the accident. Before I was born.'

Nan was nodding.

'Oh, he died all right, Leo. You see . . . the thing about Tom was . . . he was an alcoholic too. Only they didn't have things like rehab in those days.

'It killed him in the end,' Nan went on. 'The drink creeps up on them, you see, slowly. They think it's their friend. They seem all happy, the life and soul of the party and all that. And then . . . and then . . . it gets them, sure as eggs is eggs . . .'

Leo felt all churned up inside but mostly he felt angry. Angry that he didn't know. And angry at Nan too.

'But, Nan! Why didn't you listen when I said about Dad? Don't you remember? I tried to tell you. Why didn't you do something?'

'I was scared,' Nan replied. 'I didn't know what to do. If I said anything to anyone, then maybe he would lose his doctor's thingummy, be struck off. It's what he said to me once, Leo. He told me that if I said anything he'd lose it all and end up like Dad . . . and it would be all my fault.' She placed a hand over Leo's.

'I couldn't do that to him, now could I? Not to my Tommy. You don't understand how well he did. How hard it was for him with your grandad dead. He was only a child when his dad died, you know . . . just a boy . . .'

Leo pulled his hand away from Nan's, his anger all too clear now.

'Oh, I understand. I understand everything. Don't

you see? The same thing happened to me. To me, Nan – to *me!*'

She held out her palms as if to stop him, her face contorted in pain.

'I'm sorry, Leo,' she said, 'I didn't know what to do for the best. It's a terrible thing, the drinking. It's a terrible thing to live with. Sometimes it's just easier to – well – pretend . . .'

Leo stood up, his anger overpowering.

'Pretend it's not happening!' he shouted. 'But it *was* happening. It was happening to *me* . . .'

Nan sat still. Her eyes fixed somewhere in the middle of the room.

'When we got married, it was fine, you see. He came home every day for his tea. He was a clever man, your grandad. Never had the chances Tommy had. Worked for the Borough, you see. Did the town's gardens. He was a gardener. Did you know that?'

Leo shook his head. There was so much he didn't know.

'We weren't much, Tom and I. Poor as church mice, we were! He loved his flowers, though. He always brought me flowers, did Tom . . .

'And I had my little Tommy. We were happy, we were . . . so happy, until . . .'

Nan closed her eyes, casting her mind back, trying to remember.

'I can't remember when it went from the normal

kind of drinking to the alcoholic kind. I suppose there's a line, isn't there?'

She opened her eyes and looked at Leo. She reached out for his hand again.

'I expect you know that already. Don't you . . .?'

Leo saw something then, saw it in Nan's eyes. He knew what it was. It was the feeling of pain.

'I don't know when Tom crossed it. But cross it he did. And then . . . and then he stopped coming home for tea so much . . .'

Nan leant forward and started to play with Leo's hair, twisting it between her fingers.

'And then he didn't come much at all,' she said quietly. 'And then one day this policeman came and knocked on the door. He was with this WPC. Nice she was. Ever so kind.

'They said he wouldn't have felt any pain. They said he was so drunk he'd just walked into the road. They said – what with this and that . . . what with the drink – that it was bound to happen one day. Something like it. You know . . .'

Leo didn't know what to do or what to say. He squeezed Nan's hand.

'We never talk much, do we?' she said, trying to be more cheery. 'Is there anything you want to ask your nan? Anything. Anything at all.'

Leo thought for a moment, wondering if this might be his only chance.

'Why did you hate my mum?' he said finally.

'Oh, love . . .' Nan began. 'I didn't hate your mum but I . . . I had to protect my Tommy, didn't I? I mean when they split up, you see. I had to side with flesh and blood.

'I was worried, see – worried about Tommy.'

Nan sighed.

'She had the look of you, did your mum. She was beautiful, was Sarah . . . A bundle of energy she was, just like you. Always on to the next thing. She always had a list of things to do. Crossing things off and adding things on . . .'

She looked up, her tears drying now.

'You know what I think?' she said. 'I think she'd be very proud of you.'

Nan and Leo sat together, her arm stretched around him, cuddling up.

Outside it had begun to rain again. The drumming on the window panes familiar and comforting.

Chapter 19
Finding Out

It wasn't till Leo was tucked up in bed that he remembered he hadn't checked the computer.

He made a mental note to do it in the morning. He'd Google Paul Mariner too, he thought. Check him out.

Funny about Dad having an England shirt too! Even if the shirt was weird-looking.

Leo smiled and pulled back the covers. He was still wearing Dad's shirt and shorts and they'd have to do for bed.

He thought about Nan and what she'd said about Grandad. How the accident wasn't what Leo had always thought it was: just an accident.

Leo began to worry about Dad too. He'd had an accident, hadn't he? The fire. Would he be so lucky if he had another?

Sleep came in fits and bursts.

It was night when he woke in the middle of dreams and thought he could remember them. But then, as he lay in the dark, the dreams ebbed from his memory, just out of reach.

He seemed to lie awake for hours unable to sleep. Then, later, he would wake with a start from a deep sleep but know he had not really slept for long at all.

Then Leo remembered being woken by birdsong. It was early. Outside it was still dark but he knew the day was breaking.

He couldn't get the picture out of his mind, the photo of Mum and Dad.

Leo sat up in bed, trying to remember the expressions on their faces.

But he could not. All he could remember was the feeling that Mum and Dad were very happy. That they were happy just being with each other, like other people's mums and dads.

He remembered the white towel dressing-gowns. He remembered the colour of the sofa they were cuddled up on: a deep red.

There was something else too. Something niggling him.

He was sure – as sure as ever he could be – that he had switched off the light in the hut.

And yet, when he'd looked back, there *had* been a light. Under the door.

He pictured the string cord that hung next to the door. He remembered it had a big knot on the bottom, like the one in Nan's bathroom.

It made a solid sound when you pulled it on and off. Like the sound you make when you click your tongue on the roof of your mouth.

Leo got up and went over to the window. It was getting light now. Cars parked around a tiny green. In the middle a wooden seat facing out in a hexagon shape around a sapling. One day a tree. He tried to count the sides of the bench. How many sides did a hexagon have?

He rubbed his eyes. He was awake now, his mind abuzz. There was no way he was going back to sleep.

He crept to the door and across the landing towards the stairs.

Leo had made his mind up. He would find his shoes and a coat and go back to the hut. He wanted to look at the photo again. To have it. He couldn't believe he'd left it behind.

He pictured the exact place he'd put it. It was in the top drawer. In the chest in the hut.

As he tiptoed down the stairs, he saw the computer and remembered.

He hadn't read his emails.

He checked the clock above the fire. It was still not half past five. As long as he was quiet, he had loads of time.

Leo switched on Nan's PC and it burst into life. He grimaced at the noise but just as quickly the computer was quieter, booting up.

He would need a coat for his walk to the hut. He decided to have a look in the cupboard under the stairs.

When he opened it up, there was a row of coats. Old-lady coats. He pushed them along, looking at them, one by one. At the end there was a coat that looked about his size, with a sort of fur bit around the edge of the hood like an Eskimo's. It was wearing thin now. The coat was getting old.

There was a name-tag in it, like the ones he had for school.

T. RAKE

Of course!

It was Dad's coat from school.

Leo grabbed it and went into the kitchen to find his shoes and the key to the hut. He'd put the shoes on, he decided. He needed to be ready for an early escape.

By the time he sat back down at the computer he was ready for the off. He could escape at any moment. One footfall on the stairs and he'd be out the door and away.

The coat rustled every time he moved. But there was no way Nan would hear a sound as low as that.

Leo reckoned he wouldn't need a password and he was right. Nan had it set up just like Dad's account. All he had to do was keep clicking through.

He found his portal. He tapped in his password.

There were two unread emails. And they were both from the Prime Minister.

Leo clicked on the first. It was amazing. He'd actually replied straight away but Leo just hadn't checked.

Flora was right! He was going to come and open the library.

He glanced at the stairs. Had he heard something?

Quickly he clicked on the second email. He saw it had been sent more recently.

From: primeminister@gsi.no10.gov.uk
To: leo200@mac.com
SUBJECT: MANDERS
Dear Leo,
Just a quick message. You didn't reply to my last email . . . maybe you didn't get it? You can never tell with these things here.

I rang Mrs Turner. I am coming on Friday 19th. If you don't hear it officially don't worry. They won't announce it until the day you see, because of the security, so only you and me know at the moment.

Mrs Turner says you've had to go to hospital. She said there was a fire. I hope you'll be well enough to come and see me.

I'm supposed to be making a speech about the economy when I get there. Have you heard that the world is in a big crisis? There are a lot of very clever people here and they want me to announce a 'ten-point plan' to save the economy. That's what we do in the government when we have a big problem, we come up with ten points and call it a plan.

But shall I let you into a secret? One you mustn't ever let on about.

They've only come up with six points! They've had to go back to the drawing board to find the other four!

There's something else I wanted to mention. I want to thank you, Leo. Your email reminded me of home and how we can both see our mums even though they've passed away.

If I'm late on the big day, you'll know where I've been. I'll have been putting some flowers on my mum's grave.

One more thing! Mr Manders. Don't worry, I have a plan . . . Not a ten-point one . . . but a plan just the same!

That's all for now,

Barnaby

Underneath was some kind of automatic sign-off in a different font:

Rt Hon Barnaby Green MP PC
Prime Minister of Great Britain and Northern Ireland, First Lord of the Treasury and Minister for the Civil Service

Leo leant back and breathed out hard. Wait till they all heard about this! The Prime Minister *had* emailed him back. Him! What was it Manders had called him? An idiot? He couldn't help smiling as he logged out and bent down to switch the computer off.

Paul Mariner! He'd forgotten all about him.

A floorboard creaked upstairs. He'd have to Google him later.

Nan's house had no garden at the front. When Leo opened the door and walked out, he was straight on to the path and on his way.

It was raining, a sea mist over the town.

Leo gently pulled the front door until it closed. He took a few paces and looked back. How pretty Nan's house was really, he thought, its sky blue colour contrasting with the next house, painted pink.

What was it about Easthampton and colours? The houses were just like the beach huts. Vivid colours that made you feel happy inside.

Ordinary places weren't like this. They were much duller. Leo knew that. And things were looking up, weren't they? He was getting on with Nan. And now even the Prime Minister was emailing him.

When he looked up, he saw the lighthouse looming above. Of course! He'd forgotten Nan's house backed right on to it.

It towered over the sleeping town, its pure white rounded walls unblemished, perfect.

And behind the lattice glass at its top the red light slowly turned.

It was raining steadily. Leo pulled up his hood and walked methodically, his eyes fixed firmly on his shoes. He was on the seafront now – all he had to do was choose one of the ways down on to the promenade. He'd reach the hut in minutes.

As he walked, he wondered why he was going at all. It had begun to pelt down with rain and the wind was ripping in from out to sea. He glanced to the end of the pier, spotting the early-morning fishermen braving the salty dawn.

He knew he wanted to see the photo and Mum's painting again. But there was something else too. Something drawing him back.

When he got near the hut, he stopped. Something had changed.

Was it the sea?

The water was flat now, becalmed, except for the ripple from raindrops. Out to sea, clouds crowded on the horizon.

Leo edged towards the hut. Its brown scruffiness a sad contrast to its brightly coloured neighbours.

He cast his eyes over the names, written in proud lettering.

Corner Hut.

Gun Hill.

Lion's Den.

Then Leo remembered what the other thing was, the thing he'd wanted to check.

He'd wanted to check the light under the door.

The gap at the bottom of the hut doors was a centimetre or so. Leo walked up the small steps, got down on his hands and knees and looked underneath.

He was sure it was dark inside. He felt for the key in his pocket.

The door opened more easily this time. For a moment Leo stood still in the gloom.

The white string with the knot on the bottom swung gently from side to side.

Leo reached out and pulled it. A satisfying plasticky sound.

Click-Clunk!

The light came on. A lone bulb hanging from the hut roof. A cobweb clung to the white cord above it.

He switched it off and on again.

Click-Clunk! Click-Clunk!

Leo glanced around the hut, his eyes settling on the chest of drawers.

The photo was where he remembered. When he took it out, he stared at it, examining every detail, looking for clues.

The dressing-gowns had posh blue writing on them in a kind of spirally hand. Big loops like a girl's handwriting. He peered at the picture and tried to make it out.

The Carlyle.

He turned the photo around. There was writing on the back. And a date.

Just Married. So what if we can't afford the Carlyle! Our honeymoon. New York City!!

Underneath it said: *The Rakes!*

New York City! He didn't even know Mum and Dad had been to America.

It was like Nan often said. Sometimes you thought you knew everything. But in fact you knew nothing at all.

The rain was stopping, the pitter-patter on the hut roof slowing into drips and drops.

But Leo didn't care. He had his treasure. He remembered Mum's painting too and took it from the chest. He went outside into the sunlight, clutching his haul.

It was then that Leo saw it.

For the first time in his life, Leo saw the line.

It was there – pencil thin – just like Mum had said it was.

Out to sea, the clouds had disappeared and the deep blue water stretched forever, until it met the blue of the sky along the broad horizon.

Chapter 20
The Counting's Over

Leo counted down the days to the Prime Minister's visit. There was a whole week and two days to go.

He'd learned something about time: that if you wanted it to go fast it sort of seized up and stopped. The best thing to do was not think about it. If you could.

'The doctors say you can stay at home with me to look after you,' Nan said the day he went to check the hut. 'But if you go gallivanting off again, there's a hospital bed waiting for you, mark my words.'

There'd been some good news too.

'If you rest up, I reckon you'll be back at school in time to see the Prime Minister,' Nan said to him one night when she was laying the table for the next day's breakfast. 'I know how keen you are on him.'

Leo was going to explain that he'd written the letter inviting him to open the library. He was even going to explain about the emails. But he thought better of it and kept quiet.

Finally the big day came round. The days were longer now, and Leo woke way before it was time to get up.

At first he thought it was sunlight that woke him. But then he heard it again.

Thwack!

Something had hit the bedroom window!

Leo jumped out of bed and looked outside.

Thwack!

Outside he saw somebody bending down, looking for another stone to throw.

It was Flora!

Quickly Leo undid the window-latch and pulled up the window.

'Flora! Have you gone mad?' he said, his voice a hoarse whisper. 'What on earth are you doing?'

There was something comic about the way Flora froze, a fresh pebble between her fingers, her arm ready to swing and throw.

She lowered her arm.

'Sorry!' she said, beginning to giggle. 'I couldn't sleep.'

Behind her the toothpaste white of the lighthouse stretched into the morning's milky sky.

'Why didn't you ring the bell?' Leo whispered.

Flora really was beginning to giggle now.

'I didn't want to wake people up,' she said, a little bit loudly.

She pointed at the door.

'Let me in!' she said.

Leo crept downstairs and began to undo the locks on the inside of the door.

There were so many. There was one where you just turned a knob. One with a key on the inside and finally one with a small chain with a round end that slid into a slot.

'It's like Fort Knox in this house,' Leo said when he finally opened the door.

'What's she got in here? The Crown Jewels?' Flora mocked, taking off her school shoes and putting her bag down near the door.

'No. But she has got a lot of knick-knacks,' Leo said quietly, trying not to laugh.

He waved towards the porcelain animals sitting on the window-sill. There was a hedgehog. A pig. Two cart-horses but no cart. And a sheepdog.

'Come in the kitchen, love,' he said, doing his best Nan impression. 'Shall I put a brew on?'

Flora laughed a little too loudly once again, only stifling her laugh by putting hands over her mouth.

She pointed at the table already set for breakfast.

'Expecting someone?' she chortled.

This time it was Leo who laughed too loud.

'Ooooh . . . can't be too careful,' he said in his sing-song Nan voice. 'You have to be prepared, love!'

There was a voice from the stairs.

'Taking the mickey out of the old and infirm, are we?'

It was Nan. She was up!

'Mrs Rake – I'm – I'm ever so sorry. It was my fault –' Flora began.

Nan rounded the corner and came rolling in like a ship in full sail.

But she was smiling.

'Listen, young lady – don't you think I can remember the days when I was so excited I couldn't sleep? I haven't always been such an old sourpuss!'

She reached out and tousled Leo's hair.

'Anyway,' she said, 'I expect you've been wondering why Leo couldn't go out. He needs looking after, you see. Feeding up.'

Nan gave Leo a once-over.

'You will put your vest on today, like I said?'

'But, Nan,' Leo said, 'it's nearly summer.'

Nan smiled at Flora.

'He's missed you, you know. He won't tell you that, of course, because he's a boy.'

Nan winked at her.

'They never tell you. Mind, I bet you've missed him too, haven't you? He's very handsome, isn't he –'

'Nan!' Leo protested, noticing Flora's face going red. 'We're excited about the Prime Minister.'

It was Nan's turn to laugh now.

'Well, you don't say,' she chuckled, lifting up the

kettle and glancing at both of them. 'What is it I say, Leo: "Shall I put a brew on?"'

Nan impersonating him impersonating her was too much for Leo.

'Come on,' he said to Flora. 'There's something I want to show you on the computer.'

He glanced at the clock.

'We've got loads of time.'

They sat for a while waiting for the computer to boot up, then Leo went to his Favourites and clicked.

A page came up.

'Who's Paul Mariner?' Flora said.

'Ma – rin – *er*!'

They both turned to the kitchen.

'Ma – rin – *er*!' Nan sang again in her high-pitched voice, her head appearing round the door. 'It's what they used to sing at the Town – well, it's what Tommy used to sing anyway. You know, when he was your age.'

Flora looked from Nan to Leo, not understanding.

'Tommy?' she asked. 'Who's Tommy?'

Leo laughed.

'Tommy's what she calls Dad, see.'

Flora smiled.

'And this Mariner is . . .'

'Paul Mariner. Ipswich and England. Tommy's – I mean Dad's – favourite.'

Leo turned back to the computer.

'Look,' he said, 'I found this on YouTube. It's from the World Cup. England versus France 1982.'

A small picture came up on the computer. A football stadium. Men in shirts just like Dad's.

A commentator in high excitement.

'Ray Wilkins coming in here . . . And Francis and Trésor's missed it . . .

'It's been driven in by Paul Mariner! He couldn't have asked for an easier chance!

'Mariner scores in his fifth consecutive international . . .'

The picture froze on the screen.

'Told you!' Nan said from the kitchen. 'Ma – rin – er! That was him. Loved him, your dad did.'

Leo turned to check Nan was still in the kitchen. He grabbed Flora's arm.

'That's not all. Have a look at this email. Guess who it's from!'

Flora looked puzzled.

'From *him*. You know. Him that's coming – today.'

'You mean, the Prime Min–'

'Shhhh.'

They both turned towards the kitchen.

'Ma – rin – er.' Nan was still happily chanting to herself as she worked.

Leo logged on and clicked through to the email, watching Flora's expression turn to astonishment as she read.

'Breakfast's ready,' Nan trilled. 'You better get a move on or you'll miss the big day.'

When they went into the kitchen, the TV was on. Nan was watching the local news.

'Well, it's a big day here in Suffolk today and a big day especially for the children of Pier Road Primary School in Easthampton,' a lady behind a desk was saying. 'We're going over now to Mel Moloney, who is outside the school gates.'

Leo leant forward and turned up the sound. A tall black-haired lady was on the screen now.

'Look!' he yelled. 'Look. It's our school!'

'Yes, Abby,' the lady began. 'I'm here at a school with a secret it's been keeping until this morning. Later today, here in Easthampton, Pier Road Primary's most famous pupil is coming back to open a new library – and that pupil is none other than the Prime Minister, Barnaby Green.

'With the world economy in a state of crisis, Mr Green is expected to use the occasion to deliver a major speech on getting us out of this mess. According to today's *Financial Times* newspaper, he will announce a new ten-point plan –'

Leo and Flora looked at each other and began to laugh.

'*SIX*-POINT PLAN!' they erupted in unison.

Leo was laughing so much he nearly fell off his stool.

'Shhhhh!' urged Nan. 'What has got into you two? Listen . . .'

The reporter was continuing.

'I'm joined here by the brains behind today's big day. The man who had the idea to invite the Prime Minister back to Pier Road . . .'

Leo and Flora exchanged glances.

'. . . he's also someone who remembers the young Barnaby Green very well because he taught him, giving him his first helping hand up the greasy pole of life. The Prime Minister's first teacher, Malcolm Manders . . .'

'WHAT?' Leo shouted out.

'Shhhhh!' Nan said a second time. 'Have some respect – isn't that your teacher?'

'But . . . But . . .' Leo said, not knowing where to start or how.

The lady was smiling at Manders as if *he* was the Prime Minister.

'Mr Manders. You've dreamed up a great plan here! Can you tell us how you had the idea?'

'Had the idea!' Leo interjected again. Flora touched his arm.

'Just listen,' she whispered.

Manders filled the screen.

'What *is* he wearing?' Flora said under her breath. 'I've never seen him in a suit before . . .'

It was true. Manders had dressed up specially.

Gone was the red roll-neck. Instead he looked like a businessman on the telly. Dark suit, blue shirt and matching tie.

'He's had a makeover!' Flora laughed.

'Shhh!' Leo urged. 'He's talking!'

But when he began to speak, he didn't sound like Manders at all.

'One has ideas, doesn't one . . .' he began. 'I wanted Barnaby to come back, and the opening of the library – well, one thought that was the perfect moment –'

'Who does he think he is – Prince Charles?' Flora said.

'Barnaby was a great reader. I always remember Barnaby saying a book . . . a book was to him a hidden discovery, something to – well – to . . . discover.'

The pretty interviewer had another easy question.

'And you taught the Prime Minister, didn't you? Can you tell the viewers, Mr Manders, what he was like as a pupil?'

Manders scratched his beard.

'One doesn't like to betray confidences,' he said, glancing at the camera. 'After all, young Barnaby has gone on to very big things –'

Leo had stood up. He was fuming now.

'Oh, do shut up!' he shouted at the TV. 'Barnaby didn't like you! Nobody likes you!'

Nan was having none of this.

'"Barnaby", is it? A friend of yours, is he? How about we shout less and listen more? You better get him off to school, Flora, before I change my mind. *Barnaby* indeed . . .'

Nan leant over and switched to another channel. Another lady was talking to the camera and *she* was in the school playground too.

'And we will be joined later by the teacher who taught Mr Green, Malcolm Manders of Pier Road Primary School in a little town called Easthampton . . .'

Leo turned to both of them, astonished.

'That's breakfast TV, *national* breakfast TV – it's not even local. He's making himself famous and it was all *my* idea!'

Nan clicked the telly off.

'You don't half talk some rubbish,' she said. 'Now let's be having you. Come on. Off you go!'

By the time Leo and Flora turned into Pier Road he had begun to calm down.

'You and your nan seem to be getting on fine,' Flora said. 'I thought you didn't like her, but she seems OK.'

'Funny you should say that,' Leo said quietly. 'I was thinking that earlier. You know, when she was making us breakfast. She's all right, is Nan.'

They stopped walking.

'She's changed, you see. She . . . well, we've had

some nice chats. She told me all about Grandad. It was why she didn't talk about Dad.'

'Grandad?'

As they made their way to school, Leo told Flora all about Grandad and how he had been drunk when he'd been run over – and how everybody had covered up.

Flora seemed animated. He could tell she had questions bubbling up.

'That's horrible. Your poor nan,' she said.

Leo realized he hadn't thought about Nan's feelings much.

'But if your grandad was a drinker,' Flora carried on, 'then why didn't she realize about your dad?'

They could see the school now and were walking towards it. There was a great big van outside, parked on the double yellow lines, with a white satellite dish on top and a mass of aerials. Behind it was another one, just the same.

'She said she was scared they'd stop Dad being a doctor. She said he might have got – you know – struck off.'

Flora was shaking her head.

'You seem like you're on her side, though. I mean, she was so rotten to you . . .'

'It's not that,' Leo said. 'It's like with you and your dad. You know. When you talk about it all, things seem to make more sense. Nan was just like me, really. Wasn't she? She was just covering up.'

A helicopter hovered in the sky just above the school.

'And your dad? Is he coming home?'

Leo shrugged.

'I guess so. But we're nowhere near moving back into the big house yet. Nan says he'll be away for ages.'

'But he will come back, right?' Flora asked.

Leo peered up at the chopper in the sky, its rotors cutting the air.

'I'm beginning to wonder if he wants to – come back, I mean,' he said.

'But he's bound to, isn't he?' Flora said.

'Your mum doesn't live with you, does she?' Leo replied. 'She went away, remember? Just like Dad went away before . . . Only he came back that time. Maybe, this time, he's had enough of me.'

'But you miss him, don't you, Leo?' Flora said.

Leo didn't reply straight away. Instead he had stopped still. He was thinking.

'I think I miss him,' he replied eventually. 'I do. I just don't want to miss him too much, you see, in case he doesn't miss me.'

They had reached the school gates now. All around them cameramen struggled with equipment. Leo saw the reporter he'd seen interviewing Manders. She was drinking coffee from a polystyrene cup.

And in the middle of the playground was Manders himself, talking to yet another TV reporter.

Leo could just catch what the teacher was saying as they passed behind him.

'A friend of Barnaby's?' He was preening. 'Well, one doesn't normally want to talk about these things, you know . . .'

Chapter 21

Barnaby's Return

The Prime Minister's official black Jaguar sped through his old school gates, two leather-clad police outriders acting as motorcycle escort.

Barnaby Green leant forward eagerly, looking out. He felt like a time traveller.

Everything about his old school was the same, but everything was different. Pier Road seemed somehow smaller, his younger life dwarfed by the new. Was it that he was bigger? Or did it all look 'small town' by comparison?

Barnaby squinted through the car window at the official party.

There was always an official party.

Adam Harlow, his press secretary, leant over, appearing to read his mind as he always seemed to. Harlow's job was simple. He was there to tell the Prime Minister what to say.

Sometimes it seemed to Barnaby that Harlow may as well *be* the Prime Minister.

'Official party is: Pamela Turner, Head Teacher; Malcolm Manders, one of the teachers; and then the Head of the School Governors, a Mr –'

'What about Leo Rake?' the Prime Minister said slowly, interrupting Harlow. 'Don't you remember, I said I'd like to see Leo Rake?'

The press secretary eyed his boss suspiciously.

'A Mr Rake? Sorry, boss, you've got me there. Maybe he's one of the invisible Rakes, eh?'

Barnaby glared at him.

'He's a pupil,' he snapped back. 'You remember those. They have them at schools.'

The Prime Minister leant towards him.

'You *did* go to school, didn't you, Adam? Or were you born knowing everything?'

Harlow grimaced, looking down at his papers.

'You need to snap out of this mood, boss. We're already running ten minutes late. They're all here, you know –'

He jabbed his finger at the satellite trucks. 'This is a big speech. Maybe your biggest ever. We can't miss the bulletins.'

Harlow shrugged his shoulders as if the bulletins were nothing to do with him. He tapped his watch. 'Time waits for no man . . .'

'You may recall, the reason we are late, Adam, is that we stopped by the cemetery so I could put some flowers on my mother's grave.'

Even Harlow didn't have an answer for that.

Barnaby peered through the Jag's thick bullet-proof glass at the three people lined up.

'See that man in the bad suit?' he mused, glancing back at Harlow, who he noticed wasn't really listening. 'He used to teach me. He teaches Leo now too.'

Harlow was grinning. 'Well, maybe he'll have more luck with this mysterious Leo – one out of two ain't bad.'

Barnaby examined Harlow. He wanted to ask him how he'd got to be so rude – whether it was a gradual process or whether, one day, he'd just woken up the rudest man in the world.

And why was it, Barnaby wondered, that rude people seemed to run everything everywhere? It was something he'd noticed since he'd become Prime Minister. Was it because they shouted loudest? He was pretty sure it was.

Barnaby had another question. This one out loud.

'You know what I hate?' he asked.

Harlow grinned.

'Me?'

'No, apart from you, Adam. Everybody hates you. Even your kids. Even your cat hates you, I'm sure.'

The Prime Minister paused to consider the Bobster. He summoned up his furry face in his mind's eye. It was something he always did at times of great stress. He found it made him feel better.

'Have you got a cat, Adam? At home, I mean. That is, if you ever *go* home?'

'I hate cats,' Harlow said. 'Can't stand the things.'

'Thought so . . .' Barnaby whispered under his breath. 'Only the good people like cats. It's a rule of life.'

Harlow pretended not to hear again.

'Tell me what it is then, boss – what you hate . . . but hurry up. They're circling – the media's out in force, you know. Big day for Barney-boy! Today's the day you've got to save the world. Remember?'

'I hate pomposity. It's what people do to cover up failure. Just like Manders over there. Look at him. Standing to attention.'

Harlow smiled weakly.

'He used to scare the hell out of me,' Barnaby said, his eyes narrowing.

Harlow grinned smugly.

'Well, he shouldn't scare you now, boss,' he said.

'You know, I think I've spent my whole life proving that man wrong . . .' Barnaby said quietly.

Harlow continued, like a deaf bull in a china shop.

'Final check, boss – are you OK with the speech?'

Barnaby tried to run through the highlights in his mind.

'Yes. You want me to talk about why I loved the school and then . . . then I solve the global economic crisis in ten minutes flat. Isn't that about it?'

Harlow grinned mischievously.

'It's all on the autocue. All set up as normal. Read what's on the autocue, OK? Don't think about it: just read. Then cut the ribbon, a quick hello to the kids in the school hall and we're outta here – OK?'

The noise of helicopters above them was suddenly deafening.

'School hall?' Barnaby shouted above the noise. 'I thought I was opening a library?'

Harlow was checking his notes.

'Looks like they couldn't fit the whole school into the library so the gig's in the hall. You just have to cut a ribbon when you're done.'

Barnaby glanced up at the helicopters. They were news choppers. They hung menacingly in the air.

One was so close, he could read what it said along its side.

All the News. All the Time.

'The trouble with news all the time is that sometimes, just sometimes, I haven't got anything to say,' he sighed. 'Do you know what the worst thing is about this job?'

Harlow puffed his cheeks. 'No tips?'

'No. No silence. I am never allowed to say nothing.'

'Well, you're going to have to say something today,' Harlow smirked, 'because by my reckoning we've got every network and every newspaper from America here, let alone London. This is PRIME TIME, me old mate. The world is in meltdown and it's Barney-boy to the rescue.'

Barnaby turned to get out of the car.

Harlow grinned again, adding: 'Oh, boss? One more little tip for the day. Forget the kiddies. None of them can vote. You have to be eighteen, remember!'

'Very funny,' Barnaby whispered sadly. 'They'll all vote soon, you know. And when they do I have a feeling we're all going to be in a lot of trouble.'

Harlow shrugged his shoulders.

'Don't sweat it, boss,' he said. 'You'll be long gone before these geniuses get a chance to vote in elections.'

Barnaby thought, not for the first time, how much he disliked Harlow.

Four security men in black suits jumped out of a black Range Rover immediately behind them, muttering into small black microphones that hung off their ears and dangled in front of their mouths.

'There they go . . .' Barnaby said under his breath, '. . . the little black-dot men.'

Another black-dotted man jumped from the front of Barnaby's own car and opened his passenger door with needless urgency, talking rapidly without a break into his mike.

Before he emerged, ready to meet and greet, Barnaby turned back to Harlow and whispered,

'These guys and their microphones. What do they talk about? They never stop.'

Harlow smiled smugly.

'They talk about you, boss. Haven't you worked that out yet?

'The whole world talks about you.'

Leo stood watching the scene from a window in the school hall, his face pressed up against the glass by the weight of other kids behind him.

'He's getting out!' Flora shrieked. 'Look at all the TV cameras behind . . .'

They were all supposed to sit waiting on the benches that had been put out specially. But with Manders standing outside, the children couldn't resist crowding round the windows.

The Prime Minister went down the official line one by one. He hardly said a word at all to the first man, then Leo saw him smiling at Mrs Turner. They chatted for quite a while.

Then Mrs Turner turned round. She was pointing towards the hall.

The Prime Minister was in animated discussion now. He was smiling and even laughing. Leo noticed another man standing with him. He'd got out of the Jag too.

This second man was taller. He kept looking at his watch.

The class began to murmur. What was going on? Mrs Turner seemed to be talking to Manders now. Leo noticed the Prime Minister had folded his arms.

He seemed to be waiting.

'Ohmigod!' Mary Chesterton shouted suddenly. 'Manders is coming!'

Leo glanced at Flora. Sure enough, Manders had begun to walk back towards the hall. Staying where they were, the PM and Mrs Turner were peering after him.

There was something about Manders, though, something in his manner.

'Look at him,' Leo whispered. 'Something's happened. He's absolutely fuming.'

It was true. Manders was a picture of anger. His face was puce.

BANG!

Manders threw open the hall door. He'd pushed it so hard it smashed back against the wall. Papers from a noticeboard fluttered to the ground in protest.

He wavered back and forth, his ridiculous frame filling the door. It was as if Manders couldn't find the words to say. Seconds ticked by, a minute even, and still he dithered.

When he spoke, it was in his usual mocking tone.

'There has been, as they say, a change of plan,' he boomed. 'The Prime Minister has a small

215

announcement he wants to make before he makes his speech.'

Manders nodded towards the school stage, all set up with the waiting autocue and microphone.

Leo glanced behind Manders. The scene was pure chaos!

Everybody was queuing up to get in – Barnaby Green, the tall man (who was looking confused), an annoyed-looking Mrs Turner, another man Leo didn't recognize, and then the TV crews, loads of them, jostling cameras and their great furry microphones.

Mrs Turner thrust a finger towards Manders.

'Well?' she said in her loudest voice. 'Have you passed on the Prime Minister's request to the children?'

'What on earth . . .?' Flora whispered. The packed hall was silent.

Manders cleared his throat.

'Er . . . No . . . Sorry, Mrs Turner. I explained the change of plan and said the Prime Minister had an announcement –'

Manders gestured towards the PM, who was casting his eyes around the hall, as if he was looking for someone he knew.

'– I can hardly believe what he asked for,' Manders hissed, his hand uselessly covering his mouth. 'I mean, does he really want to –'

'Just say it!' the headmistress said sharply, jabbing her finger again.

Manders cast his eyes heavenwards and tutted, as if it was all a joke.

'Is Leo Rake here?' Manders mumbled.

He had the look of a defeated man, like his team had just lost on penalties in a cup final.

'Louder please, Mr Manders,' Mrs Turner said.

'Mr Rake? Are you here?' Manders asked, this time so everyone could hear.

Leo hovered by the window, thinking about putting his hand up.

He looked at Flora. Was it the email he'd sent? he thought. Had what he had said about Manders got him into trouble?

His stomach knotted.

Then another voice spoke. A very well-known voice.

'It's just that I wanted to say hello.'

It was the Prime Minister.

'Only,' he continued, 'when I said I wanted to see Leo Rake, Mr Manders here said he wasn't at school today.'

Barnaby shot Manders a look. Mrs Turner looked at the floor, embarrassed.

'Even though he was here for the register,' she rasped, glaring at Manders.

It was the Kerry girl who spoke up first.

'He's here, Sir! Over here. By the window,' she yelled.

'Looks like he's really done it this time,' Mary Chesterton chimed.

Flora elbowed Leo.

'Put your hand up,' she whispered.

Slowly Leo raised his hand. He could hear his heart beating.

'Here, Sir!' he said, as if he was answering the register. It was all he could think of to say.

Leo watched as the entire school, standing between him and the hall door, turned round and stared.

Then something extraordinary happened. The Prime Minister began to walk through the crowd of kids, who simply parted, awestruck, as he walked.

Manders fussed behind him.

'Move out of the way for the Prime Minister, please . . . Come on . . . Make way . . .'

When he had got through the mêlée, the Prime Minister walked towards Leo, his arm outstretched.

He seemed so famous Leo couldn't believe he was real.

'You must be Leo,' the PM said, shaking his hand with a firm grip. 'I'm Barnaby.'

The Prime Minister's face, known across the world, grinned.

The whole school was turned towards Leo, who went bright red and lowered his head.

When he glanced up, Leo saw that the tall man had emerged from the crowd. He looked even more hassled than before.

'Mr Harlow. Do you mind?' the Prime Minister said, the camera lenses fluttering behind him. 'I'm talking to my friend Leo here.'

Harlow ignored him. He always seemed to ignore him.

'We'll miss the lunchtime news. You need to make your speech now.'

Harlow jerked his head towards the TV cameras. 'They're here for a reason, remember!' he whispered.

Barnaby smiled at Leo and winked.

'If it's OK by you, Mr Harlow, I don't think I'm going to make that speech. I'm going to make a different speech.'

Harlow froze.

'A different speech,' he said slowly, glancing at the TV cameras. 'You haven't forgotten, you know, *them* . . .'

'Oh, I never forget *them*. How could I? With you around?'

Barnaby leant closer to Leo. 'Do you know what an autocue is?' he said, pointing at the black stand with a glass screen on top of it that stood on the stage. 'It's a machine that tells me what to say. Me? I'm *supposed* to be the Prime Minister, but all I do is parrot whatever that machine tells me to.'

He straightened up and directed a determined look at the tall man. 'But not today, Mr Harlow, not today. Today is a different day.

'All I need is that,' he said, pointing to the microphone stand.

Leo made to turn away. 'Don't go, Leo,' Barnaby said. 'Come and join me on the stage.'

He looked around.

'And you, Mr Manders, I'd like you to come up with me too, just for old time's sake.'

Barnaby cleared his throat. There was silence throughout the hall.

'Speech about to start,' a black-dot man croaked in military staccato. 'Then party will be exiting to playground and departure . . .'

Casting one quick glance behind him to where Leo was sitting, the Prime Minister began.

'Today is a very special day for me, a day I have put off for far too long. The day I returned to Easthampton and to Pier Road Primary, the school where I learned so much.'

He paused.

'There is somebody here I would like to thank. Thank from the bottom of my heart.'

Manders, sitting on his chair behind the PM, was preening again. He straightened his tie and glanced at Barnaby, doe-eyed, like he was a little bit in love.

'I want to thank one of the pupils here. His name is Leo Rake. You see, it was Leo who asked me to come and open the library. If it hadn't been for him, I wouldn't be here with you all today.'

There was a gasp throughout the hall. Leo looked at Flora, who was sitting in the front row. She had clasped her hands together as if to applaud.

But the Prime Minister was only just hitting his stride.

'I also want to thank Leo for something else. Something very precious.

'I want to thank him for reminding me what's important in life.

'You see, when I look at Leo here, I see myself looking back. He reminds me of what I was like when I sat here, on these benches, in this hall.

'I remember what it was like being a pupil at Pier Road Primary. I remember the dreams I had, but I remember too that being a child isn't as easy as the grown-ups like to think. I remember the feeling that I wasn't as good as the other kids, the feeling of being different from everybody else.'

A photographer crouched in front of Leo and aimed his camera at him.

Flash!

Leo was blinded by the light. But the photographer wasn't finished.

Flash! Flash!

'Leo and I have a couple of things in common too,' the PM continued. 'The first is that we both had wonderful mums, mums who aren't here to see us –'

The PM's voice seemed to lose its richness, becoming reedier.

'Well, to see what became of us. To see . . . what kind of people we are.'

He regained his composure, his familiar voice returning.

'The second is that we were both taught by the very same teacher, Mr Manders here.'

Manders simpered. He straightened up like a peacock.

'You see, when I was your age, nobody ever thought I'd make anything of my life. I wasn't a star like they say I was now. I wasn't really up to much at all. Even my school reports weren't up to much.

'Just ask Mr Manders here. *He* remembers. In fact, he was the one who told me.'

Manders, however, was suddenly looking blank.

'He's forgotten, you see. He can't remember what he said. Can you, Mr Manders?'

The hall was silent. The Prime Minister had grabbed the microphone from its stand and had turned to Manders, like a host on a TV show.

'You said I was a waste of space, that I'd never amount to very much at all.'

Manders stared ahead. He had begun to tremble.

Barnaby turned back to the hall. 'So do you know what I did? I set out to prove Mr Manders here wrong. I wanted to prove *everybody* wrong. I was quite determined, you understand.

'Mr Manders had quite an effect on me, he did. I used to think: "Just you wait and see, Mr Manders – one day, *one day*, I will be important; I'll be a success."

'And do you know what? I succeeded. I went to a university as old as the hills – older really – where they've educated more Prime Ministers than you can shake a stick at. I became a lawyer. I made a fortune. I made so much money I need never work again.

'But I had a plan, you see, a plan I'd started to hatch in this very hall. I turned to politics. By the time I was thirty-five, I was in the cabinet. Then, last year, I made it. I not only achieved my ambition, I topped it . . .

'I walked into Ten Downing Street the youngest Prime Minister in years – centuries, even. They said I was . . . let me remember now . . . Yes – they said in the papers I was the brightest man in politics for a hundred years.

'But do you want to know the truth?

'When I closed the front door at Number Ten, I felt as alone as I did when I used to sit in this hall. It didn't make a scrap of difference. Not really.

'Because it's what's in *here* that matters . . .'

The Prime Minister was pointing to his own head.

'It's whether you're happy inside. Whether you're *really* happy.

'If you spend your life proving other people wrong, you might just find they never cared in the first place. Just like Mr Manders here! He doesn't even remember . . .'

The Prime Minister walked over to Leo and put a hand on his shoulder.

'Then this boy taught me a lesson. He reminded me what it was like to be a kid, to be a son. To have to cope when things don't go your way.

'And he gave me a chance to come back here to tell you all, to tell the whole world, what I have learned.

'Happiness doesn't come from money or having a big job. It doesn't even come from fame. They can all be nice things, but they're not the main things.

'When you grow up, some of you may be successful – whatever that means – but the important thing is not what other people think of you: it is what you think of yourself.'

Leo shot a glance at Harlow. He sat slumped in a chair in the front row, his head in his hands.

'Don't live your lives just to prove people wrong.

Live them for yourselves. If somebody happens to offend you, let it pass. Try to relax. It isn't easy – in fact, it's really hard.'

The noise of the news choppers was growing louder. In the hall the cameras whirred, the shutters flickered.

The Prime Minister was finishing now. His voice grew quieter.

'They're listening to this all over the world,' he said. 'They were expecting me to talk about the economy. But I didn't want to talk to you about money. I didn't want to talk about ten-point plans.'

He winked at Leo. Then Barnaby's gaze turned to the crumpled figure of Manders.

'But I'm not worried about what anyone else thinks any more.'

The PM placed the microphone back on the stand. He stood tall and proud, his face bursting into a smile.

'Shall I tell you the truth, Pier Road Primary? Shall I level with you?'

He smiled at Leo.

'I haven't got all the answers. All I can be is honest, say what I really think.

'Like, I miss my mum. Like, I'd swap every bit of my success, every last bit, for one more chat with her. One last conversation . . .'

The PM was ending now.

'She used to tell me to be myself, did my mum. And do you know what? She was right!

'So I shall be myself. If I don't have an easy answer to a problem, from now on I shall say so.'

The PM looked over at Manders, whose face had gone the palest white.

'And if the answer doesn't please certain people . . .'

He glanced again at the cameras.

'. . . I shall say it anyway.'

Leo began to clap, then Flora clapped too. Applause began to spread across the hall, getting louder and louder.

'Thank you, Pier Road Primary!' the PM shouted above the clamour. 'And thank you, Leo Rake. For giving me a second chance.'

Chapter 22
The Man in the Drive

It was summer by the time Leo and Nan moved back into the big house. By then everyone had begun to forget all about the day the Prime Minister came to Pier Road Primary.

The reporters didn't leave town straight away, though. They followed Manders, waving their tape recorders, and one even came and knocked on Nan's front door.

But it didn't last. One by one they eventually moved on to the next big happening, and you could walk down the High Street and not see a single TV news crew interviewing a single local. Easthampton was just plain Easthampton once again.

The funny thing was, though, that Barnaby Green became more popular than ever after that. People seemed to like a Prime Minister who told the truth.

It even seemed to suit him.

Leo and Nan liked living in the big house. They

did the garden together, making it like it used to be.

They even started to visit Mum's grave together. Leo liked that. Remembering. One day Nan bought him a wind chime just like the ones near Mum and they hung it in the rose garden.

Whenever it chimed, it reminded him of Mum.

He felt like he was growing up too. Nan would run errands back to her house and leave him in charge. He liked that.

One summer's evening, Leo was just changing for bed when Nan said she was nipping back to the house to do the garden there.

Leo leant out of his window and watched her go. It was a perfect evening; the sun was still high and he could hear the sound of the waves on the beach.

He gazed at the garden. The roses were in full flower now. A mass of pinks and reds and whites. There were other flowers in the garden too. Small ones. Yellow and white, growing through the grass.

He'd noticed the chamomile coming up a few weeks ago. He'd even picked some of the flowers and dried them out in his bedroom.

When he'd harvested enough, he and Nan were going to make some chamomile tea and even show the pot to the angels, just like Mum had taught him to.

Leo heard a car door slam. The noise of a departing vehicle.

Whoever it was had stopped at the little gate.

When he looked down, he saw a man standing at the end of the drive. He was carrying a suitcase in one hand while the other was gripping some kind of plastic bag, like he'd been shopping.

At first Leo didn't recognize the man. But then he realized who it was.

Of course . . .

It was Dad.

Leo was sure it was Dad. Only, this dad was a different dad. He was thinner, all slimmed down. Even his face was different, like it had been hewn out of an older, fatter face.

At first Leo wanted to run down the stairs straight away. He wanted to hug his dad.

But instead he hesitated. Something was holding him back.

Leo put his head out of the window and tried to shout.

'Dad!'

He didn't seem to hear.

'DAD!'

Then all Leo felt was dizziness. He closed his eyes and just heard the sounds.

The muffled thud of the suitcase being dropped.

The squeak of the gate as it opened. The crunch of feet on the gravel path.

Then the footsteps on the stairs.

Only these footsteps weren't like before. They were lighter, quicker. They weren't the thumping crashes of the old dad.

But what kind of dad was coming up the stairs?

Did he even *know* this dad?

Leo stood up as if to greet a stranger. The door opened slowly.

Dad's skin was different. His cheeks glowed pink.

His eyes were different too. They were a pale blue and the whites weren't latticed with red.

Dad was trying to smile – Leo could tell that – but he couldn't mask a nervousness.

He was holding out the shopping bag, which swung slowly to and fro.

'I . . . I bought you a present . . .' he said softly.

Leo could see what it was as soon as he took the bag. Quickly he took out his gift.

It was a brand-new football.

'I thought maybe we could play pyjama football,' Dad said in his new soft voice. 'Maybe not tonight – you know, if you don't want to . . . but soon?

'You remember, don't you? When we used to play pyjama football?'

Leo wanted to say so much, wanted to tell Dad he was always thinking about the happier days, that he had never forgotten a thing.

But he just nodded.

'Nan? Is she home?'

Leo shook his head. 'She's gone out. I don't think she'll be very long. Dad . . . what's this?'

Dad was holding out an envelope that he had taken from the bag.

'The place that I've been to, the place that's made me better –'

'You mean Promise?' Leo said, eyeing the envelope. It looked familiar, somehow.

Dad smiled.

'Yes. Promise,' he said. 'I'm glad you know about that.

'Well, when I left today, they gave me all my things, including this. But it's addressed to you.'

As Leo took the envelope, he felt the hairs go up on the back of his neck.

Of course it was familiar. It was the letter from Mum! The letter he had lost in the fire.

He stared at the writing on the front. He could only just make it out behind the sooty smudges.

Mr Rake, it read.

Mister?

Surely the letter was for Dad?

Then Leo looked more carefully. There was a letter next to the name, between the *Mr* and the *Rake*. The letter *L*.

But he could see why they had thought the letter was for Dad.

All Leo wanted to do was to rip it open and read every word. But not here, not in front of Dad.

After all, it was private. It was *his* letter.

He'd sneak down the garden as soon as he could and read it there.

Dad sat down on the bed, smoothing it with his hand.

'Come and sit down here,' he whispered. 'There's something I want to say to you.'

There was something else different about Dad, something that made Leo happy inside.

It was when Dad put his arm around him and pulled him close that he remembered.

It was the way he smelt. He smelt like the dad he could barely remember. The dad before Mum was ill. The dad that didn't ever seem to drink.

He smelt of fresh air.

Leo wrapped his arms around him, the letter in his hand, stored up safe for later.

When he looked up at him, he saw that Dad was getting ready to say something important.

'You and me . . .' he said. 'We're just going to have to start again.'

Then Leo began to cry. But they weren't sad tears, they were happy tears. And somehow it was OK to cry now. Somehow it didn't matter any more.

'I've got . . . I've got . . .' he mumbled, his face pushed into Dad's new smells.

'What is it, Leo? What have you got?' Dad said.

Leo spoke the faintest whisper.

'I've got my daddy back.'

Leo looked up at Mum's room from the garden and ran his hands across the precious envelope.

Dad was getting changed. Leo wondered if he was putting on his PJs.

Maybe he'd come bounding down the stairs just like he used to. Maybe pyjama football was back already.

He held the envelope up to the summer's night, the only sound the glassy music of the chimes from the rose garden.

There was something written in the top right corner. *18th*.

Leo shuddered. He remembered how Mum had put the birthdays in all the corners.

This was the letter from Mum for his eighteenth birthday.

That's why she'd called him 'Mr Rake'.

Leo began to open the envelope, pushing his index finger under the seal, breaking the paper.

Something made him pause.

Was this right?

Was he supposed to open up a letter meant for when he was eighteen?

It wasn't that he was frightened. Nor was he even

nervous. It was just that he wanted to do the right thing. He didn't want to let Mum down.

Then Leo thought about his old life. Night after night of hiding Dad's bottles. How he fell asleep at school and always had the wrong kit.

Wasn't he practically grown-up already? He remembered what the Prime Minister had said about him in his speech.

Leo gathered himself. Then he spoke out loud. 'I'm ready now.'

He opened the envelope and pulled out the letter. Only it wasn't a letter, it was a handmade card, with a picture on the front.

It was one of Mum's pastels. It reminded him of the picture they'd found in the skip, only this one just had one kind of flower in it: her favourites, chamomile flowers, growing in lush green grass.

Leo felt the prickling of memory.

His own voice in his mind.

'What's *Anthemis nobilis*, Mum?'

Then his mother's voice. That day in her room.

'When I'm gone . . . you know, Lion; when I am no longer here . . . They will remind you of today.'

He reached down and picked a chamomile flower from the lawn, turning it slowly in his hands.

'*Anthemis nobilis* . . .' he whispered.

Leo opened up the card. There was writing on both pages, small and tight.

There was a date at the top. At first Leo didn't
register it at all, but he knew he had to concentrate.

He must read it slowly. Take it in.

After all, this was the only letter from Mum. The
only one he'd ever have.

Leo let his wet eyes move up and down the letter,
registering the date, taking in the year, the month,
the day.

When he realized, he froze at its awful familiarity,
a date he could never forget. A date burned into his
memory forever.

It was the day his mother died.

My Darling Boy,

*Happy eighteenth birthday, my darling Lion. As I write this,
you are just a little boy. I am upstairs in my room and I can
hear the sea and the noises of the shore. It is morning and
I'm alone with my chamomile tea and my thoughts.*

And, yes, I did show the teapot to the angels!

*I hope you liked the other birthday cards. Have you kept
them somewhere safe? Each one was a message from my heart.
But they were meant for a child, not a grown-up.*

*But today you are an adult. Your childhood is in the past
and now I can talk to you as a grown-up. I can tell you things
I've kept secret up to now, things you need to know.*

*My strength is running out, my darling. But there is so
much I need to say to you before I go.*

You need to know some truths too. Truths about Dad.

Your dad is not a bad man, Leo.

He loves you with all his heart, just like he loves me.

Your dad always drank. Most grown-ups do and for most of them, that's OK.

But for Dad it wasn't OK. When he started to drink, he couldn't stop. It had him, Leo, the alcohol had him in its grip. It overpowered him, you see.

It changed him. It drove him inside himself. He put up the shutters and ran away to be alone. At first he was just alone inside his head and then, eventually, he left us altogether. It was a terrible thing to see, Leo.

I tried so many times to help him. He knew he had a problem but he wasn't ready to admit it.

He was not ready in my time.

Do you remember what I said about faith, Leo?

I have faith. I have faith that things will be OK, in the end. I feel it strongly, even now.

Love is faith really. It's all tied up together. It is putting your trust in someone or something without all the evidence. It's a leap in the dark . . .

Sometimes you have to take those leaps. Sometimes you have no choice . . . You have to hope.

Hope that Dad will be ready in your time. Hope that, one day, you will see the better Dad.

He didn't always crash about the house and shout and yell. His eyes weren't always red from drink.

Once there was a different dad. A wonderful dad.

A dad who danced with joy the day that you were born.

You should have seen his eyes, Leo. They were as clear and blue as the sky.

I hope one day you'll see the blue in Daddy's eyes.

Try not to go Dad's way, Leo. Look at the joy in life.

Try to love yourself, whatever faults you may think you have.

I want you to do something for me, do it every day,

Count your blessings not your problems. Try writing them down every now and again.

It sounds crazy, I know, but it works. Some days you will be sad because of me or because of other things that come and go. When that happens, write down the good things and think of them.

Decide to be happy, Leo. Life really can be as simple as that.

Remember that as I sit here I am happy. I am happy because the world is beautiful. I am surrounded by my books and by my memories.

And I am happy because I have a beautiful boy.

So decide to be happy. Don't do it for me, do it for yourself . . . do it for my grandchildren. Do it and see what happens . . .

(Here the ink changed from black to blue and the last bit of handwriting was hard to make out. It was smaller now and pushed together. Like Mum had been writing in the dark.)

It's time for me to say goodbye. I am very close to the end of my life now.

But I'm with you, Leo. Watching over you.

I am there in the sea, my darling, and in the sky.

I am in the dazzling.

And remember the flowers, Leo. Always remember the flowers.

Look to the garden and you will see me there.

Acknowledgements

Thanks to: my wonderful parents, BW, Peter Cox at Redhammer, Dr Maggi Dawn, Francesca Dow, Helen Fraser, Jason Gissing, my editor Sarah Hughes at Puffin, Prof. John P. Kotter, Dr Robert Lefever, Simon Oakes, P, Alan Parker, Alison Poole, Helen Scott Lidgett, Dennis Stevenson and Max Yelland, the boy who invented pyjama football.

Author's Note for Younger Readers

When I finished writing this book I sat back and suddenly realised what it was. It was the story of what might have happened to me and my son if I hadn't stopped drinking alcohol. I am not the father in the novel. But I came close to being exactly like him or even worse. In 2005 I stopped drinking in the same way Leo's dad did.

Many of you will drink alcohol when you grow up, just like I did. It may be all right for you. But for some people alcohol causes more problems than it's worth. If that ever happens to you, remember Leo's story. Remember his dad's. You will know what to do. I stopped drinking the stuff years ago and thoroughly recommend life with a clear and peaceful head. The world is quite beautiful enough without having to change your mood.

See *www.childline.org.uk* for more info and for help if you or a member of your family has a problem with alcohol or another drug. If you want to talk to a grown-up in total confidence call ChildLine on 0800 1111.

He just wanted a decent book to read ...

Not too much to ask, is it? It was in 1935 when Allen Lane, Managing Director of Bodley Head Publishers, stood on a platform at Exeter railway station looking for something good to read on his journey back to London. His choice was limited to popular magazines and poor-quality paperbacks – the same choice faced every day by the vast majority of readers, few of whom could afford hardbacks. Lane's disappointment and subsequent anger at the range of books generally available led him to found a company – and change the world.

'We believed in the existence in this country of a vast reading public for intelligent books at a low price, and staked everything on it'
Sir Allen Lane, 1902–1970, founder of Penguin Books

The quality paperback had arrived – and not just in bookshops. Lane was adamant that his Penguins should appear in chain stores and tobacconists, and should cost no more than a packet of cigarettes.

Reading habits (and cigarette prices) have changed since 1935, but Penguin still believes in publishing the best books for everybody to enjoy. We still believe that good design costs no more than bad design, and we still believe that quality books published passionately and responsibly make the world a better place.

So wherever you see the little bird – whether it's on a piece of prize-winning literary fiction or a celebrity autobiography, political tour de force or historical masterpiece, a serial-killer thriller, reference book, world classic or a piece of pure escapism – you can bet that it represents the very best that the genre has to offer.

Whatever you like to read – trust Penguin.